"Where Did You Get this Money?"

His savage tone made Tamara look over her shoulder. He was standing by the coffee table holding her purse in one hand and bills in the other.

"What are you doing in my purse? You have no right to go through my things!"

"I want to know how you came by this money! And don't lie to me, because I saw you in that hotel this afternoon! I wondered what you were doing for money, and this afternoon gave me a pretty good idea!"

"I earned it!" Tamara flared.

His nostrils widened to drink in an angry breath as his mouth curled in a sneer. "I'll just bet you did!"

Janet BAILEY

The Hostage Bride

Harlequin Books

TORONTO • NEW YORK • LONDON
AMSTERDAM • PARIS • SYDNEY • HAMBURG
STOCKHOLM • ATHENS • TOKYO • MILAN

The
Hostage
Bride

Chapter One

"Is something wrong, Tamara?" Mr. Stein looked at her anxiously through the tinted lenses of his glasses.

"No." Tamara James shook her head in quick denial even though her world was spinning dizzily. If she hadn't been sitting down when he'd made his announcement, her legs wouldn't have supported her. As it was, her pale complexion had grown even paler from shock. "It's just... such a surprise. You never mentioned that you were considering selling the company. You didn't so much as even hint that..." Her voice trailed off—she was worried that her horrified astonishment might make him suspicious.

"I used the wrong word. It's actually being classified as a merger. It isn't even official yet—and won't be until the final papers are signed," her employer explained. "Naturally Rutledge wants it kept hush-

8 THE HOSTAGE BRIDE

hush until that time. You know how the stock specu-
lators would leap on any news related to Taylor Business Machines.''

''When . . . when will that be?'' Tamara tried to get
a grip on herself and respond with her usual calm
efficiency.

''When will what be?'' The short, thin man frowned
absently at the question, his keenly intelligent mind
having already dismissed any subject that was clear to
him.

''When will the final papers be signed? How soon
before Taylor takes over?'' In her mind she was wondering how long she would have.

''The contract agreement is being finalized now by
the attorneys. All the terms have been agreed on, so
it's only a matter of taking care of a few minor details. I imagine it will be within the month.'' Mr. Stein
shrugged, as if the exact date was unimportant.

Within the month. The phrase crashed through her
mind with the force of a deathblow. Tamara felt sick
to her stomach, a nauseous pain hammering at her
head. She glanced at the account sheets and ledger
books on her desk, avoiding eye contact with her boss
so he wouldn't see the stricken look of frantic desperation in her blue eyes.

''I wish you had mentioned it before.'' Her weak
response was barely more than a whisper.

''Rutledge asked me to wait until we had ironed out
the terms. He didn't want a lot of premature rumors
flying around, and I agreed. Now that the merger is a
certainty, I explained to him that I had to inform my
key employees, like yourself. After all, we are going to

have to have a final audit of the books to close out Signet Machines as a separate entity and begin the change-over in reporting.'' He made it all sound very matter of course, which to him it was.

''Will this...Mr. Rutledge be doing the final audit?'' Tamara asked, swallowing the sickening rush of fear.

''Gracious, no!'' Mr. Stein laughed in hearty amusement. ''Bickford Rutledge is the president of Taylor Business Machines. He's the son of the founder's daughter, Alisha Taylor Rutledge. No, the final audit will be done by you, the same way it always has. Naturally someone from his accounting staff will assist you in transferring everything to their system and aid you in the audit.''

''I see,'' Tamara murmured, but she killed the foolish hope that her secret might remain hidden.

Her less than enthusiastic response to his announcement kept nagging at him. ''Something is bothering you, Miss James. What is it?''

She took a deep breath, her gaze making several ricocheting attempts to meet his concerned look. She had to tell him. From Harold Stein she was assured of obtaining understanding, but the impersonal machinations of a big corporation wouldn't be receptive to her explanations.

''I am...concerned about this merger,'' Tamara admitted, and removed the pencil from the sleek, platinum strands of her hair near her ear. Her fingers fidgeted with it as she tried to find the precise words to explain her situation. ''You know how ill my mother is, and—''

"Ah," he interrupted in sudden understanding. "You are concerned this will affect your position, aren't you? You needn't be, Miss James. Rutledge has assured me there aren't going to be any drastic changes. Part of the terms of the agreement is that Taylor will maintain any employee who has been with me for more than four years and keep them for at least a year. So you need have no fear that you will be discharged, Miss James. I have praised your efficiency and loyalty, stressed how very conscientious you have been in your work, and made them aware of your flawless work record. Rutledge indicated to me that there would be no change in your position or salary. If anything, your benefits will be increased, since you will be working for a large corporation."

His praise wasn't reassuring because he didn't have all the facts. "That's very kind of you, Mr. Stein," Tamara began, but got no farther.

"Kind?" He scoffed at her adjective. "It's the least I could do after all the invaluable support you have given me. You don't realize what a very vital part you play in this company. I don't know how I would have coped after my brother died if you hadn't shouldered the responsibility of this department."

"Thank you, but I—"

He interrupted her with a heavy sigh. "We both know, Miss James, that my brother was the business-man, not me. I have no skill whatsoever when it comes to managing a company. I can barely organize my-self, let alone a half dozen departments and their staffs. I knew it when Art died, but after a year and a half of supposedly being in charge, I'm convinced that the company is only suffering under my leadership.''

''Every employee has enormous respect for you,'' Tamara insisted, because it was the truth. ''You are a genius.''

''In my field''—he qualified her statement—''and my field isn't management. I belong in the back room, tinkering with the machines and testing innovative devices. As soon as Rutledge signs the papers, that's where I'll be. He admitted that the main reason they are buying the company is to obtain the patents. Naturally, it will be another expansion for them, but my patents were the key,'' Harold Stein declared without false modesty.

Tamara moistened her lips nervously. With each second that passed, it was becoming more and more difficult to tell him her situation.

''I don't think I can explain to you how relieved I am because of this merger,'' her employer continued. ''It's an answer to my prayers. You know that I considered simply closing the doors after Art died. But I realized how selfish that was. I wanted to play with my machines, not run a business. But I couldn't think of just myself. There were all these people who would be out of work. My conscience couldn't tolerate the guilt of depriving so many people, like yourself, of a job. Merging with Taylor Machines, I not only have what I want, but your jobs are guaranteed too. It's a blessing, Miss James, truly a blessing.''

''It must seem so.'' To him, but not to her. The buzz of the intercom interrupted Tamara. She answered it and glanced at her employer. "It's your secretary, Mrs. Danby. You have a long-distance call."

He grimaced and sighed, "I'll be glad when somebody takes over for me. Tell Danby I'll be right there." With short, harried strides, he left her office while Tamara relayed the message to his secretary.

When she'd hung up the phone, her hand spread protectively over a ledger book. She had known for a year that Harold Stein disliked running the company, but as head of the accounting department, Tamara had always expected that she would be consulted if he ever contemplated selling the firm. She never once suspected that a company such as Taylor Business Machines would approach him with a merger offer. Signet Machines was a lightweight firm in the field of office equipment. But she had overlooked the patents—those valuable patents.

Looking back on some of her employer's requests for information these last couple of months, Tamara could see the motive behind some of them. At the time she had thought his requests unusual, but she had blamed them on his inexperience—asking for information he wouldn't need in the course of everyday business.

If Taylor Business Machines was taking over in less than a month, she was positive some of their executives and staff would be taking an active part in the company before that. She had been so wrapped up in her own problems that she hadn't seen the warning signs. With more time, she could have taken steps to alter the situation. What chance did she have of doing it now? None. Maybe the discrepancy in the ledgers wouldn't be noticed. Or maybe if she explained what had happened to the new owners, they would understand. After all, there hadn't been any criminal intent involved.

Tamara gathered up the black ledger book and carried it to the fireproof cabinet to lock it safely inside. She had just closed the door and was turning the key when a pair of arms curved around her waist from behind and a mouth began nuzzling the slender length of her neck.

"It's almost quitting time, lover," a voice murmured. "Why don't you let me take you away from all this."

Tamara stiffened in the embrace, recognizing the voice, the insolent exploration of that mouth, and the masculine feel of the body pressed against hers. She pried apart the arms crossed in front of her and stepped coolly away.

"It happens to be a full twenty minutes before quitting time, Eddie." Tamara walked to her desk in the small windowless office. "You may not have any work to do, but I have."

"So? Leave it." Eddie Collier followed her to the desk, unabashed by her rejection of his advance. "Stein's busy. He won't be back. What's the difference if you leave early anyway? He's sold us out to be absorbed by a giant."

"Where did you hear that?" She suspected he was fishing for confirmation and she wasn't going to be the one to supply it.

"Stein paid a visit to the sales and service department before he came here," he informed her with a mocking look. "So you aren't letting anything out of the bag, my secretive beauty."

Tamara let the compliment slide past her. Eddie Collier was too free with them. His glibly complimenting tongue was a vital part of his forceful charm. Because of that, his good looks, and his salesman's refusal to take no for an answer, he was very successful at his job . . . and with women.

"You don't look exactly overjoyed by the news," he observed.

"It doesn't change my position." Her long fingers began tapping out the numbers of a column of figures on the keys of the adding machine. She noticed Eddie moving away from her desk and hoped he was leaving. She wasn't in any mood to spar with him.

But leaving wasn't his intention. Instead he walked over to pull the plug to the adding machine from the wall socket. It instantly went dead. Tamara pressed her sensually formed lips together in a thin line.

"Will you plug that back in? I don't have time for this playing around." Tamara made no attempt to disguise her irritation under a mask of politeness.

"All work and no play makes Jill very dull," Eddie taunted.

"I am very dull. Why don't you accept it?" she retorted.

"Because no one who is as beautiful as you are could possibly be dull." He ignored her request to walk around the desk and sit on the corner near her chair.

When Tamara rolled the chair away from her desk to plug the adding machine in herself, Eddie's hands captured both armrests to trap her in the chair. His brown eyes ran suggestively over the molding lines of her brown tweed jacket, lingered on the angrily beating pulse in her throat, and stopped to admire the flawlessly put together features of her oval face, wiped smooth of any expression. Ash blond hair formed a pale frame, sleeked away from her face into a businesslike coil. Neither the severity of her clothes nor her hairstyle could diminish the image of her aesthetic femininity. Long and unusually dark lashes outlined the blue of her eyes, shooting out electric sparks of irritation.

Tamara was aware of her natural beauty, which gave her an immunity against Eddie's particular brand of flattery. She had never regarded her looks as an asset or a liability. The reflected image she saw in the mirror every morning was something she took for granted. Intelligence, personality, and a sense of humor were far more important qualities to her than mere looks.

"Would you move out of my way so I can finish my work?" she requested with an impatient attempt at civility.

There was a vague, negative movement of his head. "Have dinner with me," he stated. "And we'll celebrate our incorporation into the world of the big time."

"You know it's impossible. I have to go straight home." She had told him so many times that he should have it memorized by now.

"Then I'll come home with you. We'll have dinner, a little soft music, some quiet conversation, and—"

"No, thank you." Tamara refused that suggestion abruptly. "The last time I invited you over for an evening, it turned into a wrestling match on the couch. Sorry, but I'm not interested in a repeat performance."

"But our match didn't go the full three falls," Eddie pointed out, and reached to trace a finger down her cheek to her lips. "You might have liked it the third time."

Tamara brushed his hand away. "You are about as subtle as an octopus, Eddie," she declared in disgust. All pawing hands and no finesse, she could have added but didn't. "Why don't you take the hint and leave me alone? I'm simply not interested."

"The lady protests too much," he mused.

Anger flared in her blue eyes. "Obviously it's more than your ego can stand to be rejected. You've dated every single girl who works here, and probably a few who aren't single. I am probably the only one who has not begun panting after you the first time you turned those dark eyes on me."

Something flickered in his gaze, but it was quickly pushed aside. "You need someone to take care of you, Tamara. You view life much too seriously. Let your hair down once in a while. Enjoy life and have fun." He used his most persuasive voice.

"Men. I don't need anyone to take care of me, although I know you wish I were one of those helpless females. I'm not sorry that I take responsibility seriously." She saw the expression forming on his face and hurried to kill it. "Don't say that you want to share my problems. The only thing you want to share is my bed.

I can't think of anything more boring." It was brutally phrased, but nothing else had worked.

Eddie straightened, removing his hands from her chair's armrests. "You are just saying that," he accused, his male pride doubting she meant it.

"I'm saying it because I'm tired of trying to politely tell you no and have you insist I mean yes." Tamara sighed wearily. "Nothing personal, but you turn me off, Eddie. Would you mind leaving my office? I have some work that I need to finish and I'd like to get home as soon as possible."

"Your world revolves around this office and home, doesn't it?" he murmured, standing away from her desk. He didn't look angry, but neither did he look pleased. "Somewhere you should fit in time for friends."

"I do need a friend right now, but that isn't what you are offering." Her mouth twisted wryly in regret. After Stein's shocking announcement, Tamara desperately wished for someone to confide in, but she was equally aware that Eddie wasn't the one. "Good night, Eddie." She let the farewell prompt him into leaving.

He started to go, then paused to plug the cord into the wall socket. "You'll never be lonely, Tamara. You have your work to keep you company. Maybe you have a computer for a heart."

"If it consoles your ego, go ahead and believe it," she replied with dry humor, and turned to the column of figures that needed tabulating.

"You work too much with facts and figures. Life isn't a bunch of statistics. It's feelings and emotions. You need reprogramming."

"I'll keep that in mind," she promised without looking up from her work.

When he'd left, Tamara let her fingers pause on the keys of the adding machine to stare at the door he had closed. Was she too realistic? She had to be. Life had to be faced squarely. No one was going to come along and miraculously sweep her problems away. It wasn't a rose-colored world she lived in, but she had acquired the strength to carry her burden and didn't object to the load. Eddie's line of thinking led to self-pity. Nothing would be solved by that.

However, it was true that she regretted the absence of a real friend. Over these last few years, the friendships she'd shared had withered away. It was understandable. A person had to devote time to friendships to keep them flourishing and growing, but she hadn't been permitted that time. And the giving couldn't be all on one side. She had accepted that fact without protest.

Her gaze returned to the column of figures. Just for a second, her blood ran cold with fear at the thought of the impending merger. Tamara quelled the sensation of rising panic. There would be a rational solution. Nothing was ever as hopeless as it seemed. What was the worst that could happen?—she might lose her job. With her qualifications, she could easily obtain another position as a bookkeeper. To be fired was the worst that could happen, Tamara kept insisting to herself. Harold Stein would intervene in her behalf if anything worse was threatened.

A glance at her watch started her fingers tapping out the numbers on the keys of the adding machine. But it was a quarter past five before she finished, which meant she had missed her bus and had to wait for the next one.

Impatient to be home, her restless gaze didn't notice the budding green of the trees on the Kansas City boulevard the bus took. The glinting rays of a lowering sun turned the water spewing from a stone fountain into a golden shower. It was something she saw but didn't appreciate as she kept glancing at her watch and waiting for her corner to be reached.

It was a two-block walk from the bus stop to the small, one-story house of stucco with green shutters at the windows. Tulips bobbed their heads as Tamara hurried up the steps to the door. The first blooms of the lilac bush near the house had begun to scent the air with their fragrance. There was a passing thought that her mother would appreciate a bouquet in her room before Tamara hurried inside the house.

"I'm sorry I'm late, Sadie," she apologized the instant she saw the tall, broad-shouldered woman wearing brown slacks and a cardigan enter the living room. "It was after five before I got away from the office—then I missed my bus. I hope I haven't made you late for anything."

"Gracious, no!" The woman dismissed the suggestion with a gruff laugh. "The only thing waiting for me at my apartment is the television set."

Tamara lowered her voice to ask, "How's Mom?"

A smile softened the angular features of the nurse's face. "See for yourself."

Leaving her purse and jacket on an occasional table, she walked with light, quick steps to the archway Sadie Kent had just come through. Her spirits were lifted by the sight of the thin woman sitting in a cushioned armchair.

"I don't need to ask how you feel today, do I?" Her usually composed features became animated as she bent to kiss a pale cheek. "Hello, Mom."

"Hello. How was your day?" The words were said slowly and carefully to conceal the faint slur of her speech pattern.

"Fine," Tamara lied. "What did you do today?"

"I watched my soap operas, but I am not going to bore you with their troubles." A fragment of a smile curved at her mother's mouth, but her muscles weren't able to maintain it. Yet there was a definite twinkle in her eyes, blue like her daughter's.

Each day Tamara asked a similar question and always received a similar response that dismissed any discussion of her mother's day. It had to be utterly boring to be confined in the four walls of one room, but it was typical of her mother not to complain. Only once had Tamara ever heard her mother cry out in protest. Then it had been a simple and poignant "Why?" when the doctor had informed her she had a debilitating disease that was slowly but surely killing her muscles. That had been three years and innumerable medical bills ago.

With each passing day, Tamara had observed that as her mother grew weaker, her spirit grew stronger. It was impossible to pity someone who didn't pity themselves. Her mother was a source of inspiration. As long as she didn't wail in despair, neither could Tamara.

These last few months, her mother's condition had deteriorated rapidly, as the doctor had warned them it would. She couldn't even do the simplest things for herself anymore, which was why Tamara had employed a nurse to stay with her mother while she was working.

The endless treatments, the drugs, Sadie's salary, the doctor's bill had long ago exhausted their meager savings. The house was mortgaged to the full extent of its worth. Even the inheritance her mother had received eight months ago from some distant relative was gone. Three months ago, Tamara had been at her wit's end, not knowing which way to turn, until a solution had presented itself to her. She would have to come up with another answer now, but she had been given intelligence as well as beauty. She was confident she would find it—somehow.

She pushed that problem aside for the time being. "I don't know about you, but I'm starving, Mom. Is there anything special you'd like for dinner tonight?"

"A steak, medium rare. A baked potato, heaping with sour cream. And a slice of cheesecake," her mother ordered in her carefully concise voice.

"One steak, ground and medium rare, coming up," Tamara joked. It had been so long since the grocery budget had been able to buy a steak that Tamara doubted if she recalled what one would taste like. Hamburger and stew meat was about the only beef she purchased, balanced by fish and chicken. "First, I'm going to change clothes."

"Relax awhile first. You don't have to rush right out to the kitchen to fix supper," her mother insisted.

But Tamara just smiled. She returned to the living room as Sadie was about to leave. "Thanks for staying late," Tamara offered.

"You don't have to thank me. Nurses are supposed to become involved with their patients, but you know how fond I've grown of your mother. I would stay with her for nothing." Sadie brushed away the gratitude.

"I hope the day never comes when I might have to ask you to do that." There was a painful tightening of her throat.

Sadie clicked her tongue. "Keep your chin up," she instructed sharply.

With a quick smile, Tamara obediently lifted it an inch. "See you in the morning."

When the nurse had left Tamara went to her bedroom to change into a pair of brushed denims and a long-sleeved sweater of cinnamon velour. She had managed to keep her wardrobe fairly up-to-date by paying regular visits to the bargain counters and garage sales. Ingenuity and a skillful needle and thread were usually all she required to hide material flaws or adapt a dress to the latest style. She shook her hair free of its coil to fall with leonine thickness about her shoulders. It changed her image from cool efficiency to one of earthy sensuality, but Tamara was unconscious that the transformation was in any way startling.

While the hamburgers were cooking on the grill, she helped her mother back into the bed and went back to the kitchen to prepare the tray. It was simple fare, consisting of the hamburger patty, mashed potatoes,

Jell-O salad, and creamed peas. Tamara set her plate aside to keep the food warmed while she carried the tray in to her mother and sat on the edge of the bed to feed her, since her coordination was such that she could no longer feed herself.

"Tell me what happened at the office today," her mother requested between bites.

Tamara hesitated, then decided it might be wise to lay some groundwork for what might become an eventuality. "Mr. Stein stopped by my office this afternoon to tell me that the company is going to merge with Taylor Business Machines."

Her mother looked at her in surprise. "When?"

"The end of the month, I guess." She carefully schooled her expression to conceal her inner trepidations. "It came as a complete surprise to me, too. I knew Mr. Stein wasn't happy about running the company," she admitted as she spooned peas into her mother's mouth. "To be truthful, he isn't very good at it. He never even hinted that he was considering a move of this kind."

"Will it mean a promotion for you?"

"It could." A faint smile touched Tamara's mouth. Leave it to her mother to find something good. "Or it might mean I won't have a job. The new management might sweep me out when they take over."

"Do you think so?" her mother frowned.

"It's possible. But I'm not worried about it if they do," Tamara insisted. "There is always a column in the classifieds filled with openings for experienced bookkeepers. I won't have any trouble finding work."

"That's true." There was a pause before she asked, "When will you know?"

"Not for a while. Probably not until next month."

Tamara didn't mention her employer's assurance that she would be guaranteed a job. There were certain things he didn't know. Just as there were certain things she didn't tell her mother, because she didn't want her worrying—especially about their finances. Her mother still believed there was a little left from the inheritance she had received. She didn't know Tamara had already gone through almost twice that sum, paying the various bills they owed.

Her salary and the money she earned typing nights didn't cover the mortgage payment on the house, the utilities, Sadie's wages, and the groceries. But Tamara pretended to her mother that it did, with a little left over to pay toward the medical expenses. It eased her mother's mind, and Tamara didn't want her worrying about something she couldn't help.

"I feel very guilty sometimes," her mother declared with an unexpected sadness in her usually cheerful expression. This statement took Tamara by surprise and the forkful of meat was stopped halfway to her mother's mouth. "You are missing so many of the joys of being young because of me."

"Mother, please." There was a lump in her throat that she had to swallow before she could continue. "I'm not complaining. I have the rest of my life to date, go to parties and dances." She left unspoken that she might have only a few months more with her mother, the disease was progressing so rapidly.

"I have been very blessed to have you."

Tears sprang into Tamara's eyes and she turned her head to hide them from her mother. "I certainly hope so," she declared, attempting to joke her way out of the very emotional moment.

"You are conceited." Her mother laughed as Tamara's remark achieved the desired result.

Chapter Two

"It's going to be a beautiful day." Adam Slater sighed wistfully as he gazed out the window of the car. "I wish I were spending it on the golf course."

Bick Rutledge let his gaze slide from the flow of traffic to lazily rest on the accountant's profile. "Instead of going over Signet's books with Stein's spinsterish paragon he keeps raving about."

"You sound skeptical of her ability. All the balance sheets and statements I saw looked like they were drawn up by a highly skilled professional," Adam remarked with a questioning look.

"Maybe. I'm just doubtful if Stein knows a good employee from a bad one. The company has been stagnant the last year and a half. It hasn't shown any growth since his brother died. With those patents he owns, the business should have exploded. I don't think Stein knows what he has."

"Had," Adam corrected. "You own them now. And you didn't tell him what they were worth."

"Stein got what he wanted. So did we." Bick shrugged without a trace of guilt at the bargain he'd obtained.

"Are you really going to keep his business going?" Adam studied the man behind the wheel.

"For the time being. It will serve to handle our overflow while we weed out their employees."

"You promised Stein you'd keep everyone for a year," Adam reminded him.

"I'll keep the good ones for a year, or longer. The bad ones will probably find the working conditions not to their liking and voluntarily quit." His amused glance was knowingly shrewd.

"How long have we known each other? Seventeen years, is it?" Adam answered his own question. "We roomed together at college, so I guess that must be right. Who would ever have thought back then that I'd be working for you someday?"

"I wouldn't have hired you if you weren't the best," Bick stated, and slowed the car to turn into the parking lot of the Signet Company.

"I know that," Adam declared with a half laugh. "I don't mind working for you, but I'd sure as hell hate to do business with you."

"You make me sound like a villain." His mouth quirked.

"Not that. I just could never be as detached as you are in dealing with people . . . on a business level, that is," he qualified the statement.

Bick knew what Adam meant. Usually he kept the people he employed at a distance, rarely socializing with them. Because of their previous friendship, he permitted his guard to relax sometimes in Adam's company, but never completely. Bick had learned quickly that employees tended to take advantage of friendships. So while he maintained a loose comradeship, part of him stayed aloof and wary.

He'd been born at the top, inheriting the majority block of company shares from his mother. Even if he hadn't, Bick knew he would have sought the position. The challenge of it was ample compensation for the loneliness of command that accompanied it. Bick didn't consider himself to be an autocratic ruler. He was equally capable of joking and drinking with his men as he was giving them orders.

"Where are we going to start our tour?" Adam asked when Bick parked the car in a stall reserved for visitors.

"Might as well look over the sales department first. Hank's already seen it, but I'll be expected to put in my appearance there," he murmured dryly.

As he stepped out of the car, a transit bus pulled away from the corner. His attention was automatically transferred to the slim blond, who had obviously just gotten off the bus and was walking toward the main entrance. By the time Adam joined him, the girl was ahead of them. A whipping wind was plastering her blue cotton skirt to the back of her legs, suggestively outlining the slender curve of her hips. Bick would have been less than honest if he didn't admit to liking what he saw.

Her steps slowed as she appeared to be looking through her purse for something. They had nearly overtaken her when she dropped a set of keys onto the sidewalk and stooped to pick them up. As she straightened, the silk shawl that had been draped around her shoulders slipped to the ground. Bick reached for it before the summer wind could sweep it away.

When she turned around, he felt his senses stir. She was a stunning creature—such blue eyes—and he'd bet his wallet the pale blond of her hair wasn't the result of a bleach bottle. Her lips started to part in a smile of gratitude, then stopped. As she took the shawl from his outstretched hand, Bick let it trail through his fingers when he released it. Somehow he knew her skin would be just as smooth beneath those clothes.

"Thank you," she murmured.

He liked her voice—a low, silken sound. Bick knew he was staring, but he couldn't do anything about it. He inclined his head in brief acknowledgment of her words, but she was already turning to open the door. He was too late to open it for her, and followed her through before it closed.

"Excuse me, miss." She stopped when he spoke and turned hesitantly to face him. Out of the corner of his eyes, Bick saw the glass-walled partition and the assortment of office machines beyond it, but he deliberately ignored it. "Which way is the sales department?"

"Right through that door." She pointed to the glassed area, a set of keys jingling in her hand when she did.

His gaze ran admiringly over her, noting the thrusting firmness of her breasts and the nipped-in slimness of her waist. "What is your name?" When his gaze returned to her face, it encountered an impenetrable wall of reserve. Her studied indifference immediately intrigued him even more.

"I'm sure you'll find someone to help you if you step through those doors." She coolly ignored his question and pivoted on a slim heel to walk away.

Adam exhaled a long breath beside him. "I never thought I'd live to see the day you would get the brush-off, Bick," he murmured, then added to himself, "I wonder if I should tell Peggy that I finally met her."

"Met who?" Bick dragged his gaze away from the retreating figure to let it narrow on the head of his accounting staff.

"Oh...uh." Adam faltered as he realized he'd spoken aloud. "Peggy made me take a quiz that was in this magazine," he explained, referring to his wife. "One of the questions asked if I had ever been unfaithful. I assured her that I hadn't, because I'd never met a woman who had ever tempted me. But that one"—he glanced down the hallway where the blond had disappeared—"could lead me astray."

"Forget it," Bick stated.

"Why?" Adam smiled at him curiously.

"Because if she goes out with anybody, it's going to be me." But as he said the half-joking sentence, Bick knew that he meant it.

"I thought you...uh...made it a rule never to—"

"You just saw the exception," Bick interrupted, his voice smooth and calmly determined.

Adam stared at him, then shook his head in a vaguely incredulous fashion. "You aren't joking."

"I rarely joke about something I want." A lazy, crooked smile slanted his mouth.

"And you always get what you want, don't you?" Adam seemed to marvel at the realization.

"My grandfather gave me a piece of advice a long time ago. He said, 'If you want to cross the street, cross it. If someone stands in your way, walk around them. If you can't walk around them and you can't persuade them to move out of your way, walk over them. But if you've made up your mind to cross the street, don't let anyone stop you.' In practice, it isn't as ruthless as it sounds," Bick concluded in a wry tone because of Adam's apprehensive expression. "Come on." He walked to the glass sales door. "Let's get all these business formalities over with."

He pushed aside the distraction of that blond vision dancing in his head. Business first, then pleasure. Bick couldn't think of a better reward to be waiting at the end of a day.

In her office Tamara discovered she was clutching the silk folds of the multicolored shawl. She smoothed out the creases in the delicate fabric caused by her tight grip and draped it around her shoulders. This time she tied the ends in a double knot so it wouldn't slip free again. A spicy musk fragrance of a man's cologne had left its scent on the shawl, a provocative stimulant to nerves still tingling from the encounter.

Closing her eyes, Tamara shook her head to clear it of the frankness that had been in the male gaze of those green eyes. It didn't do any good. She could still see that tall, broad-shouldered man in the sand-colored suit who had returned her shawl—the one whose heady scent clung to it now.

His features had been toughly masculine—browned by the sun and creased with experience. The morning sunlight had glinted on his dark brown hair to give it a coppery sheen. The strong breeze had whipped a few strands forward onto his forehead to give him an arrogantly rakish look. His mouth had been thin and firmly cut and his hand had been large with bluntly trimmed nails.

Everything about the man, from the expensive suit tailored to fit his muscled frame to the casually tamed style of his haircut, reminded Tamara of the chiseled and polished facets of a diamond. Although he showed the unmistakable stamp of refinement, it didn't change the inherent hardness of the stone.

All male, his interest in her had been obvious, and her ego had reveled in it. When he'd asked her name, the look he gave her had practically turned her bones to water. She had very nearly told him. But what was the use? If he had contacted her and asked her out, she couldn't have gone with him, for a half dozen reasons. So there hadn't been any point in encouraging him. Tamara sighed heavily.

She walked to her desk and put her purse in the bottom drawer. The swivel chair creaked as she sat down in it. Resting her elbows on the desktop, she linked her fingers together and pressed them against her mouth. No solution had presented itself to clear up the discrepancy in the company's books and the time for an audit was fast approaching. Tamara had considered altering the entry, but if that was uncovered, she would be in deeper trouble. Her empty stomach was twisted into knots of tension and had been for days, refusing food and eating her up with anxiety.

Three times she had approached Harold Stein to explain what she had done, but he had abandoned any pretense of interest in the operation of the company, from sales to accounting. He was experimenting with a new duplicating process, and he kept interrupting her to explain the significance of it if his new development worked. Unable to obtain his undivided attention, Tamara had given up without accomplishing her purpose.

What had the man wanted? The question startled her into sitting up straight. Why had her thoughts returned to that stranger? He'd asked for the sales department. Maybe he'd ordered some equipment or was planning to order some. What did it matter? Tamara took a firm grip on herself. Even if she saw him again or found out his name, what good would it do? She wasn't free. She had too many personal problems and responsibilities.

Pushing him out of her mind for the last time, Tamara reached for yesterday's account sheets in her incoming file basket. There was a great deal of work that demanded her attention. It was time she stopped daydreaming and started doing her job.

An hour later, she discovered a multiplication error on an invoice that had been mailed. Leaving her office, Tamara entered the large room that housed her office staff and walked to the desk of the billing clerk,

Susan Dunn. The room was abuzz with whispered conversations being exchanged back and forth between desks, an undercurrent of excitement in the air.

There was a vague frown tracing her forehead when Tamara stopped at the woman's desk. The subdued voices around her didn't indicate the normal exchange of gossip. It was as if some secret was racing through the room.

"Susan—" she began, requesting the plump woman's attention as she interrupted the whispering going on between the clerk and the woman at the desk behind her.

"Oh!" The woman turned to face her, pressing a hand to her heart as she laughed self-consciously. "You startled me! Have you heard?" Susan Dunn didn't waste any time.

"Heard what?" Tamara asked, somewhat warily, feeling uneasy and not knowing why.

"Two executives from Taylor are here, making a tour of inspection, I guess," the woman related. "Pam was just talking to Andy in the service department and he said he had to hang up because a couple of bigwigs from Taylor Machines were there."

A cold finger left an invisible icy trail down her spine. "No, I didn't know," she admitted, and attempted to show that she didn't attach any importance to the news. She laid the invoice on Susan's desk to show her. "You didn't double-check when you multiplied the unit price against the amount. You will have to send a corrected invoice to the customer and adjust the total on his account."

"I did make a mistake, didn't I?" the woman admitted absently and rushed back to her previous subject. "Do you suppose they'll come here?"

"I'm sure they will, but I expect we will be notified before they appear." That is, if Harold Stein thought of it.

Susan Dunn opened her middle desk drawer to take out a tube of lipstick and a mirror. She glanced at Tamara as she applied a fresh coat of red to her mouth. "We have to put our best foot forward for the new bosses, don't we?" She winked.

"Susan, you are incorrigible." Tamara shook her head in wry dismay. "Instead of worrying about your 'best foot,' I'd worry about being 'on your toes,'" As she started to leave, she reminded her, "Don't forget to correct that invoice."

"I won't."

Secluded in her private office once more, Tamara felt a shaking relief set in. They were here, which meant part of her waiting was over. She would be glad when this whole mess was straightened out and this sensation of dangling over the edge of a precipice would be ended.

For the rest of the morning, Tamara was kept abreast of the movements of the two executives through the various departments by her accounting staff. One of the girls had gleaned the information that Bickford T. Rutledge himself was one of the pair. Tamara was skeptical of that rumor. More than likely it was one of his many vice-presidents with the large firm.

Every time her extension rang that morning, Tamara jumped. She kept expecting to have the imminent arrival of her new employers announced. It didn't come. Rumor had it that the tour had become stalled in the laboratory. No doubt Harold Stein had become carried away with an explanation of how his new duplicating device was supposed to work, if he succeeded.

A knock at her door brought an impatient "Yes?" from Tamara. She was really getting tired of these progress reports. At this rate, very little work was getting done because of the constant discussion of the whereabouts of their new employers.

The door opened and Susan stuck her head in. "Pam and Rachel are going to watch things while the rest of us go to lunch. Are you coming?"

Tamara glanced at her watch, surprised to find that time had finally dragged itself around to the noon hour. "No, I'm not really hungry." She was too nervous. "And I have this work to finish." She indicated the papers in front of her.

"Do you want me to bring you a sandwich?" Susan offered.

Common sense insisted that she had to eat something. Tamara opened the desk drawer where she kept her purse. "The vending machine in the employee's lounge still has yogurt, doesn't it?" At Susan's affirmative nod, Tamara handed her some change. "Bring me back a container."

"Right away," Susan promised, and pulled the door shut as she left. Within a few minutes she was back to set a container of peach yogurt and a plastic spoon on

Tamara's desk. "I don't see how you can eat that stuff," Susan declared, making a face and shuddering. Tamara just smiled and waved the woman on her way.

The yogurt required little effort to eat, sliding down her throat with ease. Tamara doubted if her churning stomach would have tolerated anything more solid. She ate spoonfuls from the plastic container between posting entries in the columnar ledger.

Her door swung open without the advance warning of a knock and a puzzled-looking Harold Stein stepped in. "Where is everyone, Miss James?"

"Out to lunch." She dipped the plastic spoon into the yogurt and had started to carry it to her mouth when she looked up. Her gaze encountered a pair of lazy green eyes belonging to the tall, broad-shouldered man framed in her open doorway. A glint of satisfaction was in his level regard, while a hint of a smile softened the firmness of his mouth. Her breath was squeezed from her lungs as Tamara slowly lowered the spoon back to the yogurt and tried not to act at all surprised to see the bold stranger again.

Harold Stein was looking at his watch with dismay. "I didn't realize what time it was. I suppose you'd like to go to lunch?" He frowned at the man behind him in a somewhat absent fashion.

"I think *Miss James* has the right idea." The man stressed her name in a silent message that said he had learned it despite her previous unwillingness to provide him with it. "Why don't we have some sandwiches and coffee brought in? Is that all right with you, Adam?" He half-glanced over his shoulder and

Tamara noticed the coat sleeve of someone behind him.

"Whatever suits you is fine with me," the unseen man replied indifferently.

"Would you want to go back to my office?" Harold Stein suggested. "I can have Danby telephone the local deli for sandwiches."

"This is our next stop, isn't it?"

"Yes." Harold nodded as if uncertain of the significance of that fact.

Even before that question Tamara had put two and two together. She was certain that her calculation was correct. The two men with her employer were obviously the executives from Taylor Business Machines. Her palms became sweaty and her throat was dry. She knew her heart was not beating at its normal rate.

"Then we might as well lunch here," the man announced, and swung his unnervingly steady gaze back to her, "unless Miss James has some objection."

"None." That counted anyway. She rose from her chair to walk around her desk. "We'll need another chair," Tamara murmured in explanation of her abrupt movement. There were only two besides her own chair in the room, one in front of her desk and a straight-backed chair in the far corner.

"Adam will bring one," the man stated, taking charge as if from habit and turning to give the order. "Bring one of the chairs from out there when you come in."

"I haven't introduced you," Harold realized with a guilty start. "Miss James, this is Bickford Taylor

Rutledge, president of Taylor Business Machines and your new employer. This is Miss James, who handles all the accounting and such." With that duty completed, he moved from between them to walk to Tamara's desk telephone. "I'll order those sandwiches."

Tamara would have preferred to simply acknowledge the introduction with a nod, but Bickford Taylor Rutledge, the top man himself, was already extending his hand to her. She had little choice but to accept the polite courtesy.

"How do you do, sir," she murmured stiffly.

No matter how "malely" interested his expression was, Tamara couldn't visualize herself telling this man that she had borrowed twenty thousand dollars of company funds without permission and would return it as soon as her mother died. If he had been someone like Harold Stein or his brother, Art, she might have been able to confide in him. But there was a relentless quality about this Bickford Rutledge. He wasn't a forgiving man.

"When Harold was singing your praises, he neglected to mention how extraordinarily beautiful you are, Miss James." The compliment rolled smoothly off his tongue. It wasn't an attempt to flatter, but to reinforce the message of personal interest his eyes were conveying.

"Thank you." Tamara struggled to maintain a degree of aloofness. When she tried to withdraw her hand from his firm grip, he continued to hold it. But her attempt drew his glance to her hand.

"Nervous?" It was a low, one-word question, containing the inflection of an amused taunt.

Embarrassment trembled through her body at the way he had drawn attention to the moistness of her palm instead of courteously ignoring it. The backlash of humiliation stiffened her pride and permitted her to meet his probing gaze.

"Yes," she admitted.

"You needn't be, Miss James. Miss—" The pause was to prompt Tamara into supplying her first name. When she hesitated, he murmured, "I can always check the employee records."

"Tamara James." She gave it to him, along with a stiff smile.

"Tamara James." An eyebrow was lifted as he tested the name and he verbally concluded, "I like it."

Just for a minute, Tamara wondered if she was supposed to feel honored, but there wasn't time for any feeling of irritation to grow. A movement in the doorway signaled the return of the man referred to as Adam. As he wheeled a swivel desk chair into Tamara's office, she was being drawn forward to meet him by the hand that was still holding hers. Bickford Rutledge released it to let his arm curve around her waist. The action was very proprietorial and Tamara tried to take offense at it. It was as if he already owned her, body and soul. The insane part was she could summon no genuine objection.

"Adam, I want you to meet Miss Tamara James." Bickford Rutledge made the introduction since Harold Stein was still on the telephone. "Adam Slater is your counterpart in my organization," he explained to her with a downward glance that fleetingly caressed her features and added to her tumultuous emotions. While his hand remained heavily on her waist, his gaze turned to the man with the chair. "Be easy on her, Adam," he advised dryly. "She's nervous about facing her new employers."

How much of her attack of nerves was caused by this confrontation with her new employer and the rather dire situation she was in? And how much was caused by Bickford Rutledge, the man? Awareness of the hard, male frame heating her side was licking through her nerve ends. It had been years since a man had disturbed her this way, and Tamara couldn't recall it ever being to this extent.

She wondered if her cheeks were flushed, if she were betraying this purely physical reaction to his touch. With an effort, Tamara forced her gaze to focus solely on the man in front of her. She wished there was a mirror around so she could see if the mask of cool professionalism was in place.

"How do you do, Mr. Slater," she greeted him, and stepped forward to politely shake hands with him. The side benefit of her action was that she succeeded in escaping the hand on her waist.

"This is definitely my pleasure, Miss James," he countered, a wide smile splitting his face.

Adam Slater was almost as tall as Bickford Rutledge, but he was more slimly built, less muscled. His brown hair was a shade lighter than that of the president of the firm and lacked the fiery lights. His eyes were a warm brown, not the disconcerting green. There was nothing about him that made Tamara feel threatened. Not that she would describe Bickford Rutledge's attitude toward her as menacing. The danger from him was much more subtle.

Harold Stein hung up the telephone and turned to announce, "The sandwiches and coffee will be delivered in twenty minutes." He took a step forward and nearly walked into the chair Adam had wheeled into the small office. "Oh," he blinked. "You found another chair. We might as well sit down and make ourselves comfortable, don't you think?" he suggested.

As Tamara turned to follow through with his suggestion, she was facing the broad chest of Bickford Rutledge. There was very little room to maneuver around him.

"Won't you use my desk, Mr. Rutledge?" she offered, motioning to her chair.

"I wouldn't dream of putting you out." He refused and stepped to one side so she could get by him. "Finish your lunch. Don't wait for ours to arrive."

To tell the truth, Tamara wasn't the least bit interested in eating the rest of her yogurt. The only reason she picked up the cup and spoon when she sat down was because it gave her something to do with her hands.

Adam insisted that the older Harold Stein take the softly upholstered swivel chair he had brought in, while Adam sat in the straight-backed chair in the corner. That left the chair in front of Tamara's desk for Bickford Rutledge to occupy.

In his usually garrulous fashion, Harold Stein took over control of the conversation. Tamara pretended an interest in what he was saying, although not a word was sinking in. It became harder and harder to ignore the fact that she was being studied. Bickford Rutledge seemed to take an inordinate amount of interest in watching her eat, from the way she put her spoon in her mouth to the way the tip of her tongue curled out to lick away any trace of yogurt on her upper lip and even the way she swallowed. It was as if he found her eating to be a sensual thing. The thought rocked through her senses and Tamara set the almost finished container of yogurt on her desk, not wanting to provide him with any more entertainment.

His gaze flicked from the container of yogurt to her face. "Watching your diet?" he questioned in a voice that didn't seem to carry beyond her hearing. Almost immediately his eyes made a slow, assessing sweep of her figure, penetrating through the layers of clothes the way it had done before.

Strangely, Tamara could find nothing insulting in the look. It stripped, yes, but not in any way that was demeaning. There was its danger.

"No—it's simply a nourishing and inexpensive lunch," she explained.

There was a sharp knock on her door before it burst open. "Miss James, someone took my...chair." Susan finished the sentence lamely as she saw Mr. Stein sitting in it and the other two men. "I didn't know you had it, Mr. Stein." She glanced apologetically at Tamara and rolled her eyes. "I'll find another one."

"Thanks, Susan." Tamara smiled, but the way she was trying to guard her reaction made it an unnatural movement.

Before the woman could close the door, the delivery boy arrived with their sandwiches. Adam began asking her some questions—nothing out of the ordinary—and Tamara concentrated all her attention on the conversation with him.

Chapter Three

As Harold Stein drained the last of his coffee from the paper cup, Bickford Rutledge said, "I know you are anxious to get back to your project, Harold. I'm certain Miss James is more than qualified to answer any questions Adam might have."

"Yes, actually, I would like to get back," the man declared with a glimmer of relief in his expression. He stood up quickly before Rutledge could change his mind.

Tamara opened her mouth to protest. She might need Mr. Stein's support desperately before the afternoon was over. But when he had made it so plain he wanted to leave, how could she ask him to stay? The last thing she wanted to do was arouse the suspicions of either Rutledge or Adam Slater. No matter what, she mustn't act guilty. Somehow she would have to make her new employer understand that what she had

done hadn't been entirely wrong. Was there such a
thing as "a little illegal"? But until she decided the
best way to approach her new and formidable employer, she didn't want to prejudice her case, unless it
was in her favor.

So Tamara made no attempt to stop the older man
when he left her office. Adam immediately suggested
that he take a look at the company records in order to
understand her bookkeeping system before he super-
vised their audit. Tamara drew a silent breath of relief that the audit wouldn't begin today. She allowed
herself to relax slightly, which wasn't too difficult because she and Adam talked the same language.

He had pulled the straight-backed chair behind her
desk so he could sit beside her while they went over the
ledgers. Bickford Rutledge continued to sit in the chair
opposite the desk, but since Tamara was occupied, she
wasn't bothered nearly as badly by his steady regard.
He asked questions, too, which showed he was following their discussion.

"Would you mind if I removed my jacket?" he
asked her after they had been closeted in her small office for nearly an hour.

"No, I don't mind," she replied, but didn't watch
as he shrugged out of the tailored jacket.

"That's a great idea." Adam stood up to remove his
jacket and loosen the blue and gold striped tie around
his neck. Before he sat down, he unbuttoned the cuffs
of his shirt and rolled them back.

From the crispness of business suits and ties to the
casualness of shirt-sleeves, the change in attitude was
dramatic. Tamara immediately picked up on Adam's

shared enthusiasm for working with numbers. He enjoyed what he did, the same as she did. They discussed ways of incorporating her system and making an easy transition to the system used at the corporate offices. Plus, there was the payroll system that needed to be transferred as well.

When Adam inquired how the billing was handled, Tamara went to the wall of filing cabinets to show him an example rather than attempt to explain. Her gaze bounced off Bickford Rutledge, who was leaning a shoulder against a side wall while he leafed through a copy of a year-old financial statement. Her pulse accelerated under the lazy study of his green eyes. She firmly slowed it and opened a file drawer of the cabinet near the wall.

"It's good you don't suffer from claustrophobia, Miss James," Bickford Rutledge remarked.

"Yes, this office is a little small," she admitted. Never had it felt smaller than now—with him filling every inch. But Tamara didn't look at him when she answered.

When she found the particular folder she was looking for, she removed it and slid the drawer shut. As she turned, Tamara flipped open the folder and walked right into Bickford Rutledge, unaware that he had straightened from the wall.

His arm instinctively went around her waist as she careened into him. It stayed there to steady her. In consequence, Tamara was vividly conscious of thrusting outlines of his muscled thighs and hips. While one hand continued to clutch the folder, her other hand was splayed across his shirt front. Beneath it, she could feel the steady pounding of his heart. She didn't need any proof of how vital and alive he was. She could feel it tingling like an electric current through her nerve ends.

"As you said, the office is a little small," he murmured.

She sensed his reluctance to let her go as he dragged his hand away from the back of her waist and allowed space to come between them. Tamara walked to the desk. Adam's back had been to the filing cabinets, so he was unaware of the incident. She set the folder in front of him, but had a difficult time finding a concise explanation for their procedure. The contact had disturbed her.

Bick saw the quick smile Tamara gave Adam. Funny, he was already thinking of her as Tamara. Maybe not so funny, he reconsidered, remembering the softness of her body when she had blindly walked into him earlier that afternoon. If he had planned it, it couldn't have worked better. Just for a second, she had relaxed against him, letting her weight rest against him.

For some reason, she was wary of him, erecting an aloof barrier whenever it looked like he was getting under her skin. Yet she was relaxed with Adam. So her coolness wasn't directed at all men, but restricted to him. Maybe it was natural. Bick disliked playing games, though. He was attracted to her and didn't attempt to disguise it, while she seemed to guard every word and look directed to him.

He noticed her shoulder rub against Adam's arm. He found himself resenting the innocent contact and how at ease she was with Adam. It gleamed hard in his eyes. As he watched, Bick saw her steal a glance at her watch.

"Do you have a date this evening, Miss James?" Bick shot the question at her, as it occurred to him for the first time that it was possible she had a boyfriend.

Her head jerked up. The guilty light in her eyes revealed she knew she had been caught clock-watching. "No. But—"

"Good. Then you won't object to staying a bit longer than usual." His gaze sliced to Adam. "I know Adam wants to get this finished up before he starts the audit tomorrow."

"I don't object . . . if it isn't *too* late," she agreed.

Adam glanced at his watch. "I think I'll call Peggy and let her know where I am. She worries," he explained offhandedly, and reached for the phone.

As he dialed the number, he knocked over the framed photograph on Tamara's desk. Bick rescued it and glanced at the picture before setting it upright. It was a snapshot of two women, the younger one obviously Tamara. The other one looked remarkably like her, except that she was older.

"Your mother?" Bick questioned as he set the picture frame upright on her desk.

"Yes." Tamara glanced at the photograph, a softly affectionate light gleaming in her blue eyes.

"I can see where you inherited your looks," he murmured.

But she didn't acknowledge his comment. Instead, when Adam hung up the phone, she said, "I'd better make a call, too."

"We'll have to call it quits by seven," Adam announced while Tamara dialed a number. "Peggy is coming by with a fresh change of clothes to pick me up. We have some dinner we have to attend tonight." There was a mischievous light in his brown eyes when he added softly, "There's no reason why you have to stay, is there, old buddy?"

"I can think of one, old buddy," Bick murmured with faint sarcasm, and flicked a glance at Tamara. Whoever she had called, he hadn't been able to overhear the conversation. "No problems?" he asked her when the receiver was replaced on the cradle.

"No, no problems," she assured him with an indifferent shrug that appeared forced.

It seemed an eternity to Bick before seven o'clock and Adam's wife arrived. Several minutes were wasted with introductions and the usual polite exchanges that accompanied them. When he saw Tamara take her purse from the desk drawer, he walked to the door.

"I'll see you tomorrow, Adam. Take care, Peggy." He opened the door and paused. "Are you leaving now, too, Miss James?"

"Yes, I am." He held the door open for her and she walked by with a quiet, "Thank you."

She gave no indication that she expected him to walk with her and continued down the corridor toward the main entrance. His longer strides easily caught up with her, but Bick felt a little irritated by her aloofness.

"Since you worked late and missed dinner, I'd like to take you out, Miss James," he offered casually.

"It isn't necessary. I'll make note of the extra hours on my time card. That's all the compensation I require," Tamara insisted.

"But what about the compensation I require?" he reasoned. "I'm not looking forward to dinner alone. You could take pity on me."

Long, thick lashes veiled the sidelong glance she gave him. "I'm certain you can find someone to keep you company, Mr. Rutledge, with very little effort."

They were at the main door and he reached around her to open it. "I've made very little effort to persuade you to come with me. Or is someone keeping a meal warm for you?"

"No. I'll just fix something cold. It doesn't matter."

Outside the air was pleasantly cool and the morning wind had died to a hesitant breeze. "Now, you are making me feel guilty, Miss James. I've asked you to work late and forced you to miss a hot evening meal. And you won't let me make up for it."

"It was very thoughtful of you, but I must go home. Thank you, though," she added, plainly as an afterthought. "Good night."

"Where are you going?" He caught hold of her elbow when she started to walk away from him.

"Home. I told you."

Bick felt her straining against his hold in a mute resistance. In the flash of her blue eyes, he read defiance. The evening was ahead of him, promising nothing. She was beside him, which in itself was a promise of something. He didn't intend to let her slip away from him yet.

"If you won't have dinner with me, you can at least permit me to give you a ride home," Bick stated.

"I can catch the bus at the corner. One will be along shortly," she argued, but not very forcefully.

"Shortly? Or twenty minutes from now?" His mouth slowly curved into a smile as he noted the acknowledgment in her expression that he might be right. "My car is parked in the lot. A short, comfortable ride in it would surely be swifter, wouldn't it?"

"Yes," she agreed with a reluctant nod of acceptance.

"This way." With one obstacle surmounted, Bick was confident he could handle any other barrier she might place in his path. He kept a guiding hand on her elbow as he walked her to his car. "If you won't have dinner with me tonight, then have lunch tomorrow." He paused to unlock the passenger door.

Bick sensed her hesitancy before she answered. "It isn't necessary."

Another obstacle was crumbling. He hid a smile as he opened the door and held it for her. "It is. There is a little matter that has to be cleared up."

"What?" Halting abruptly, she went pale. At the same time, there was a leap of fear in the blue eyes that scanned his face.

It puzzled him. He reached out to touch the vein pounding wildly in her throat and felt its frantic throbbing under his fingertips. Desire surged through him, not a lusting one, but an overwhelming desire to protect. Her parted lips held a mute appeal for something—Bick didn't know what—but he sought to reassure them.

"Don't be afraid." He bent his head to brush his mouth across her lips.

When they quivered beneath the gentle contact, a more elemental emotion claimed him. His kiss became exploring, igniting a hesitant and almost unwilling response. Curving his hand to the shape of her slender neck, Bick resisted an urge to free her pale hair from the pins that held it in its smooth coil and wind his fingers into the silken mass. He didn't want to incite a sudden rush of vanity, not when he was making such delightful discoveries.

His hand sought her waist, then slid beneath the silk shawl up to her shoulder blades. She pliantly arched closer at its pressure until the soft tips of her breasts brushed against his shirt front, his unbuttoned suit jacket swinging open. The kiss, warm and stimulating though it was, was just a taste. He wanted more, but an inner voice cautioned him not to rush it. Bick sensed that something was holding her back, preventing her from responding as fully as she was capable of doing, so he submitted to the reasoning instinct. His mouth moved over her lips to savor the softness of them in a slow release.

Straightening from her by degrees, Bick studied her reaction through half-closed eyes. There was a vague shock when he discovered her features were expressing the same confused curiosity he was experiencing. An inner questioning of what made her so different from a half a hundred other women he'd held in his arms and kissed much more intimately? Yet he couldn't answer that any more than he could define what had made the embrace seem special.

An invisible door closed between them. Bick suddenly wasn't able to read her thoughts in her expression. Irritation flickered through him. If it was the last thing he did, he was going to shatter that poise of hers forever so she could never hide behind it again. There was a savage urge to do something about it that very minute, but he fought it down.

"I'm not going to apologize for kissing you," Bick declared in a smooth murmur. "Only for, perhaps, doing it too soon."

She seemed about to say something, but no indignant outburst came. She hadn't objected to the kiss and she was honest enough not to pretend otherwise, a rare quality indeed. Saying nothing, she moved to slide into the passenger seat and Bick closed the door to walk around to the driver's side.

After she had given him her address, Bick drove the car out of the parking lot into the street. Stopped at the corner traffic light, Tamara thought to ask, "Do you need directions?"

"No, I can find it."

"Do you live here in Kansas City?" With his attention on the changing light and the flow of traffic, she was able to study the bold lines of his profile—all hard, male angles.

"Yes."

No doubt in Johnson County, Tamara thought, and lapsed into silence to hold court over her conflicting emotions. She had known he was going to kiss her, so why hadn't she stopped him? Obviously she would have been a hypocrite to protest afterward, when she had made it plain she had enjoyed it. *Enjoyed*—it was such a tame word to describe the raw wonder she had felt.

An assortment of fast food restaurants flanked both sides of the street, clustering together to compete for trade the way they always seemed to do. Although it wasn't yet sunset, their neon lights were luring customers in.

"If I can't persuade you to let me take you to dinner, at least you can let me buy you a quick sandwich," Bick persisted.

Tamara wanted to agree. Whatever the force was that drew her to him, it was potent, but she retained a grip on her priorities and gave a negative shake of her head.

"I honestly have to go home." At his skeptical glance, she realized her steadfast determination required an explanation. She was neither afraid nor playing a game. "My...my mother isn't well."

"You live with your parents?"

"With my mother. My father died when I was small." Here was her chance, the opening to explain the extenuating circumstances that had prompted her to "borrow" the money. Somehow her tongue became all tied up in knots.

"I meant what I said earlier. I am going to insist that I take you to lunch tomorrow to make up for tonight. Agreed?" Beneath the challenge, there was a low threat.

Tamara smothered the phrase that was almost becoming redundant and didn't protest that it wasn't necessary. Instead she lifted a shoulder in an attempt at indifference. "You're the boss."

A little voice inside her head said, why not? Why keep fighting the fact that he's obviously attracted to you and make use of it? Have lunch with him tomorrow. Maybe even flirt with him a little. If he likes you, he will be more apt to understand. Why not have two aces up your sleeve instead of one? When Tamara's gaze strayed to his relentless features, another voice asked, was that wise?

"Which house?" Bick questioned, suddenly turning to catch her staring.

With a self-conscious start, Tamara realized they had reached the block where she lived. "The white one with the green shutters." Bick stopped the car at the curb in front of it. Tamara searched for the door handle and couldn't find it. "I think the car makers make a game out of changing the location of door handles in every car so people will have to play hide-and-seek to find it," she muttered.

Bick leaned over to reach across and lift the handle hidden in the armrest. His push swung the car door ajar. He didn't take advantage of the opportunity to touch her, although his face was briefly very close to hers.

Sitting once again behind the wheel, he said, "Lunch. Twelve o'clock sharp."

"Yes," Tamara agreed on a breathless note, and tried to conceal the wish that he would kiss her again. "Thanks for the ride."

His gaze watched her lips form the words with unnerving interest, but he didn't reply or attempt to stop her from getting out of the car. Tamara was conscious that the car remained parked at the curb until she had reached the front door and opened it. Once Tamara was inside the house, a tiny pain began hammering at her temples. There were so many things to think about. Not the least among them was the audit that would begin tomorrow.

When Tamara arrived at the office the next morning, Adam Slater was already there along with another older man named Fred Hastings. Somehow she had expected Bick Rutledge to put in an appearance, but he didn't. It was just as well, because it took all her skill and ingenuity to steer the audit in the direction she wanted it to go and gain all the time she could.

At half past eleven, Bick walked into her office. Outside of a "Good morning" directed to the two men, he didn't waste time with preliminaries. "Are you ready?"

"You're early." A shaft of fear went through her as Tamara mentally calculated how far the auditors would progress before she returned. Her heart thumped a little louder at the look in his vividly green eyes. It was at once possessive and persuasive, and utterly irresistible.

"A little," Bick admitted indifferently. "You two can manage without Miss James for an hour or so, can't you?" It was a statement that wouldn't tolerate a negative reply. "I'm taking her to lunch," he said, as if he'd done it every day of his life.

"Sure, we can manage," Adam replied and arched his back to relieve muscles that were cramping from sitting in one position for so long. "We'll be breaking for a sandwich in twenty minutes or so ourselves."

Bick nodded and looked expectantly at Tamara. After fetching her purse, she walked to the door he held open for her. The warm weight of his hand was on the small of her back to guide her out of the building. Tamara was conscious of the curious looks she was receiving from her staff and wondered if they were envious or whether they thought she was buttering up the new boss.

When they were outside, Bick said, "I made reservations for noon."

"Fine." It didn't occur to Tamara to ask where as he helped her into the car, since it didn't matter to her. When she was settled in the passenger seat, he closed the door. She found herself missing the firm touch of his hand and envied the steering wheel that was taking her place.

With typical feminine vanity, she lowered the sun visor to glance at her reflection in its mirror and check her makeup. The blue of her eyes looked overly bright, the result of the excited confusion churning inside her. The summer dress of flowered silk was one of the most flattering ones she owned that was suitable to wear to the office. She was glad she had surrendered to the impulse to wear it, liking the way the style was designed to subtly accent her curves. Her lipstick had faded. Tamara would have freshened the mocha rose color, but Bick leaned over to flip the visor up.

"You couldn't look lovelier," he stated and started the car.

The husky pitch of his voice warmed her blood. It didn't matter whether he meant it or not. Just for a little while, Tamara succumbed to the temptation to be a woman and forget the problems and responsibilities that had denied her the chance these last three years. Circumstances had made her suppress her own sexuality, but Bick was so definitely male that he made her recognize it. She reveled in the sensations it aroused.

Hugging the feelings inside her, Tamara let her sparkling gaze wander out the moving car window to the rawboned skyline of Kansas City shining under a high, prairie sun. They were entering the country club district, where trees abounded and the streets were adorned with fountains and statuary.

The fountains were a harmony of sight, sound, and movement. Bubbling water rushed to spray its song over a rearing horse, caught motionless in a symphony of powerful lines and perfect symmetry. Its conquering rider clung to its bare back under the deluge of the fountain's shower. The sight of it and its circle of statues were all reflected in the rippling pool of water that embraced it.

"More fountains than Rome, more boulevards than Paris—what more could a city have?" Tamara murmured.

"Yes, the City of Fountains . . . and vastly underrated," Bick agreed somewhat absently.

Tamara had never been to the restaurant Bick had chosen. It was not surprising considering the subdued elegance of its rich wood paneling and linen-covered tables. When she had been dating, most of her escorts had not been able to afford places like this.

A black-uniformed headwaiter greeted Bick by name when they entered. "Good day, Mr. Rutledge."

The man bent slightly at the waist. "A table for two or will others be joining you?"

"Miss James and I are lunching alone," Bick informed him, using her name as if to reinforce her status as someone special. His downward glance roamed possessively over her features as he added, "If anyone attempts to join us, I will cheerfully tell them to get lost."

If her breath hadn't already been disturbed by his caressing look, his statement permanently disrupted it. The waiter gave her an assessing glance before he bestowed a smile of approval on Bick.

"Of course," he agreed, and moved to enter the dining area, leading them to their table. "This way, please."

He showed them to a table in a secluded corner of the room. He pulled the table away from the bench seat so Tamara could sit facing the rest of the dining area. Instead of sitting opposite her, Bick slid onto the cushioned seat beside her. The solidly muscled flesh of his left thigh and hip burned through the thin fabric of her dress to electrify her nerve ends. Her shoulder rubbed his arm as she opened the menu the head-waiter had given to her. The hunger Tamara felt had nothing to do with food. Bick recommended the luncheon steak and she accepted his suggestion.

Bick ordered for her when the waiter came. "Would you care for a cocktail before lunch?" the waiter inquired.

"None for me, thank you," said Tamara.

Bick declined also, but ordered a liter of Cabernet Sauvignon. "Two glasses?" the waiter asked. "Yes," Bick replied without consulting her.

Wine, dim lights—all that was missing was soft music, Tamara thought, and experienced a sudden need to dispel the intimate atmosphere.

"You mentioned yesterday evening that there was something you wished to discuss with me, Mr. Rutledge," she reminded him.

"Did I?" An eyebrow arched with mock blankness. "And the name is Bick. Bickford Taylor Rutledge is too much a mouthful for anyone to say."

In her mind she was already on a first-name basis with him, but Tamara pursued her original topic rather than acknowledge the permission he had given her. "I presume you wanted to discuss my position under the new management." Or did he already know something about the money?

"How do you feel about the merger?" he asked.

"Surprised," Tamara admitted after an initial hesitation. "Who is going to be in charge now that Mr. Stein has stepped down? Will you?"

"No. I have already selected a business manager to fill the position. He'll be taking over Monday."

"That was a rather foolish question on my part, wasn't it?" she murmured self-consciously. "Naturally you'll be at the corporate offices, running everything."

"That's right," Bick agreed blandly. "Would you like a position there? If you worked there, it wouldn't be at all uncommon for us to see each other every day.

I can arrange to have you work on my personal staff, if you like."

With an effort, Tamara concealed the fact that his offer had shaken her. "I wasn't angling for a promotion."

"I wasn't suggesting that you were. Would you be interested?" he challenged.

Tamara attempted to joke her way out of an answer. "Would you be chasing me around a desk all day?"

When her half-laughing glance lifted to encounter his, her breath was taken by the green intensity of his gaze. "Would you be running?"

Her throat worked convulsively, but she couldn't manage to squeeze an answer out. The waiter returned to provide a welcome distraction as he poured the wine for Bick to sample before filling the two wineglasses with the ruby-red liquid.

Although she hadn't tasted a drop of liquor in more than three years, Tamara leaned forward to take the glass in both her hands. She crossed her legs to elude the searing contact with his thigh and made another attempt to steer the conversation to a less disturbing channel.

"This morning Adam and I were discussing the most efficient way to transfer the—"

A thumb and forefinger captured her chin to turn it toward him, his touch effectively silencing her even before Bick rubbed his thumb across her mouth. "No business discussions," he stated, and watched the liberties his thumb was taking with a glint of envy. "This is strictly a social lunch."

"It is?" Mentally Tamara was trying to decide if that was good or bad, but she seemed incapable of making the definition.

"Yes." Bick released her chin to take hold of her hand. "You have very nicely shaped hands," he observed as his fingers absently stroked the back of the one he held. "No rings. No bracelets. No necklace. Don't you like jewelry, Tamara?"

She'd sold every piece that had any value, but she gave him the same excuse she'd given her mother. "I'm allergic to it," she lied.

"Allergic to gold?" An eyebrow lifted in amused surprise.

"I think I'm allergic to the alloys they use in it," she shrugged.

"What about your watch?" His gaze slid to her left wrist.

"A leather band and stainless steel back," Tamara explained. "Very utilitarian."

"What do your male admirers give you for presents?" he questioned with a narrowed look.

Tamara was reluctant to admit that she had none because she wasn't sufficiently prepared to go into the long explanation that would entail. "Fortunately, I'm not allergic to flowers."

The waiter arrived to serve their food and Tamara was able to withdraw her hand from his clasp. The steak was excellent, but she spent more time playing with it than she did eating it. Her attention kept wandering to the man sitting next to her, the inherent strength in his large hands, and the gleaming darkness of his chestnut hair.

She sipped at her wine, but barely drank half of it. There was enough intoxication in the moment without adding more. If she ever needed to think clearly, this was the time.

Chapter Four

When the waiter had removed their luncheon plates, he had suggested dessert, but Tamara had asked for only coffee, as had Bick. With the meal over, Bick had rested his arm along the back cushion of the bench. While he had begun asking her opinion on nonbusiness-related topics, his hand had drifted onto her shoulder.

It had been easy for Tamara to talk to him up to that point, but it had become difficult for her to disassociate herself from the knowledge of his touch. When she had leaned forward to discreetly elude it, his hand had merely slipped down to the back of her ribs. In a somewhat absent fashion, he caressed her shoulder bones and let his hand wander down her spine and curve around the side of her rib cage, his fingertips brushing near the swell of her breast. He was wreaking havoc with her senses, not to mention her heart-beat.

Tamara started to say something and forgot completely what it was. She stared into her coffee cup, empty now. "It's very difficult to make intelligent conversation when you're touching me like that," she informed him with stiff candor.

He chuckled softly and let his fingers tighten on her ribs. "You surely don't believe that I'm only interested in your mind," Bick chided in deliberate provocation. "How do you think I feel? It's impossible to sit beside you and *not* touch you. In fact, it's difficult to sit here and not do more than that, Tamara."

A quiver of pure pleasure went through her at the huskily disturbed way he spoke her name. When she turned to look at him, he dragged his gaze from her lips. She was captured by the virile, passionate look in his eyes and swayed toward him. His head bent a fraction of an inch.

"Your check, sir," came the discreet murmur of the waiter.

Bick moved abruptly away, removing his hand and swearing under his breath. He scrawled his signature across the bottom of the tab and thrust it to the waiter. Then his gaze stabbed Tamara.

"Shall we get out of here?" he suggested with barely concealed impatience.

"Yes." After the embarrassing reminder that they were in a public place, Tamara had stolen a glance at her watch. It was already well past one o'clock, which meant she had considerably extended her lunch hour.

Pushing the table away from them, Bick rose first and helped Tamara out from behind the table. As he guided her out of the restaurant, his hand remained firmly clamped on the side of her ribs so that she was constantly being brushed against his length. He even maneuvered the door so they could walk through it together, as if he was determined not to let her out of his reach for a second.

Tamara sensed a coiled tension about him that she could appreciate. Her own nerves seemed to be wound as tightly as a spring. He walked her briskly to his car, helped her into the passenger seat, slammed the door, and walked around to climb in on the driver's side.

Once inside, Bick reached for her and hauled her unceremoniously into his arms. His mouth took possession of her lips and banished all her defenses, demanding that her mouth open to the invasion of his. He strained to hold her closer while her hands slipped inside his jacket to seek the support of his hard body. Nerve centers exploded under the probing, penetrating fire of his kiss. Tamara was dazed by the mad excitement pounding through her veins when Bick finally brought a halt to the relentless kiss and trailed his mouth across her cheek to her neck and ear.

"You don't know how much I've wanted to do that ever since I walked into your office this morning." The ragged edge to his voice reassured Tamara that she wasn't the only one aroused to the point of pain.

When she opened her eyes, she was blinded by the glare of the sun bouncing off the polished hood of the car. It returned some of her sanity and her hands pushed against his chest in mute resistance to his teeth nibbling at her sensitive skin. He lifted his head for an instant to let his eyes devour her face.

"My house isn't far from here. Shall we go there?" As he asked the question, his firm lips moved to tease the corners of her mouth, making them tremble for his possession.

Tamara breathed an affirmative answer against the intoxicating warmth of his mouth before a cold splash of responsibility cooled her ardor. "No." She took back her initial agreement and pulled away from him. "No, I have to get back to the office." How could she have forgotten that Adam was doing the audit at this very second? "And . . . and you undoubtedly have appointments this afternoon."

"So speaks the sensible, professional Miss James," he taunted with malicious sarcasm as his fingers bit into her neck. "Who the hell cares? I'm the boss. I'm giving us the day off. Appointments and work be damned."

She stiffened at his veiled insult. "That isn't fair, Bick."

His fingers relaxed and slipped away as he took a deep breath and raked a hand through the copper lights glinting in his dark hair. "No, it wasn't. And you are right. It's business before pleasure." The grudging admission was low and taut. "Your kisses don't exactly arouse the sensible side of a man's nature."

"Neither do yours," Tamara retorted, still feeling defensive.

"Really? You turned it off pretty easily," Bick accused.

She opened her mouth to protest, then closed it. "Believe what you like," she said curtly, and squared her shoulders against the seat to stare straight ahead.

His hard gaze bored into her for several seconds before he turned the ignition key to start the motor. It was a heavy, oppressive silence that dominated the atmosphere on the incredibly long ride to the office. Tamara felt crushed by it, but didn't know how to ease its weight.

When Bick braked the car to a stop in front of the building, her hand unerringly found the door handle. Before she could slide out of the car, his fingers were gripping her elbow.

"I'm sorry." Bick ground out the words as if he'd never said them before. Tamara remained poised on the edge of the seat, the door open, but she couldn't bring herself to look at him. "I am sorry!" he repeated angrily. "Is it so wrong that I wanted to be with you, that I wanted to spend an entire afternoon with you? I lashed out at you in frustration. That was wrong and unfair. And I admit it. And I'm sorry." He spelled it all out in concise, angry words. "Will you accept that?"

Tamara sensed it was the closest he had ever come to humbling himself. It soothed the hurt he had inflicted. She turned her head to look at him over her shoulder. "Yes."

With a groan, he leaned across the seat to press a hard kiss on her lips. Before it could develop into something deeper, Bick straightened. "You'd better go before I decide to forget to be sensible."

That desirous light in his green eyes had her spirits soaring into the clouds as she stepped from the car and hurried into the building. If Bick wanted her that much, if he cared that much, then surely everything would work out better than she could ever hope.

This feeling of confidence made it hard for Tamara to be unduly concerned about the continuing audit that afternoon. She tried to keep her feet on the ground, but she kept floating off. The only question mark in her mind was when she would see Bick again.

That was answered when she left the office at quitting time. As she turned to walk to the bus stop, a car pulled up to the curb. Tamara needed only one glance to recognize the car and the driver. She slid into the passenger seat, her heart skipping beats at the way Bick automatically leaned over to give her a quick kiss of greeting. Then he was turning the car into the traffic flow.

"Where would you like to go tonight?" He gave a sidelong look that was guaranteed to make her bones melt.

But it was his question that made Tamara swallow in apprehension because she knew what her answer had to be. "I'd like to go out to dinner with you, but I have to go home."

"Are we going to go through this again?" Bick sighed in irritation.

"I'm sorry, but I do," she insisted quietly.

Bick didn't argue as he concentrated his attention on the rush hour traffic, but Tamara knew the discussion wasn't over. He was waiting until he could devote all of his energies to changing her mind. She only wished she could let him.

In front of her house, he stopped the car and turned in the seat to face her, draping one arm over the steering wheel. "All right. Now I want you to explain why you can't come out with me tonight." His mouth was compressed into a thin line that said her explanation had better be a good one.

"In the first place, my mother isn't well and can't be left alone for an entire evening. Plus, I earn extra money by typing in the evenings and I have some legal contracts to do for an attorney who needs them by tomorrow morning. So, you see, I honestly can't go out with you," she reasoned and met his searching gaze.

"All right." He conceded that her argument was sound. "If you can't have dinner with me, then I'll have dinner with you."

His suggestion sorely tempted her, but Tamara breathed in deeply and shook her head. "I don't think that would be a good idea," she said with a wistful smile of regret.

"Why?" Bick demanded. "Who else is in the house? Do you have a live-in lover that you don't want me to meet?"

The gleam of jealousy in his green eyes kept the question from stinging. "No. There isn't any-one... any man living with me."

"Has anyone made an offer recently?" A warmth had entered both his voice and his look.

"Not recently," she admitted on a breathless note.

"Not until now," he corrected.

His mouth began a slow descent toward hers and Tamara moved to meet it. Her hands eased their way around his neck to link up and curl into the sensual crispness of the hair at the back of his neck. The silk material of her dress allowed his hands to glide over her ribs and lift her with a twisting motion until the upper half of her body was molded to his.

The long, sensuous kiss made her feel warm and weightless in his arms. His hands were spreading and shaping, flattening her breasts against his chest, the buttons of his shirt digging into her tender skin. When his mouth left hers, she tipped her head back to permit his easy exploration of her throat and the hollow below her ear. Exquisite shivers of joy danced over her skin, drawing an unconscious sigh from her lips.

Bick raised his head, satisfaction and desire flaring his nostrils before his mouth returned to seductively cover hers. Shifting, he laid her across his lap, cradling her head on his arm and shoulder. A loving languor stole over Tamara. One hand slipped from his neck to curve inside his open jacket. She could feel the heat of his hard flesh burning through the material of his shirt and the drumbeat of his heart.

The male hand that had been cradling her hipbone left it to unbutton his shirt and guide her hand inside. Her heart thudded wildly against her ribs as her fingers came in contact with the living bronze skin of his chest. A springing vee of hair tickled the palm of her hand, stimulating another moan from her throat, which his mouth muffled and absorbed.

Reduced to a state of helpless desire, Tamara felt a shameless pleasure when his hand cupped a breast, molding it into his palm and exploring its slopes and peak through the material of her dress. Her own caressing hand wandered across the hard, flat muscles of his stomach and drew a violent shudder from Bick. Forsaking her lips, his mouth moved to her ear, his tongue darting out to start violent tremors between the love nips of his teeth on her earlobe.

"My God, Tamara," he breathed against her skin, speaking with a labored effort. "I can think of a lot more satisfactory place to make love to you than the front seat of the car in broad daylight."

"Yes." There was an aching throb in her voice. "The steering wheel . . ."

"The steering wheel, the zipper on your dress—why couldn't you have worn something that buttoned down the front?" Bick criticized with mock gruffness and punished her with a sweetly hard kiss.

His hand ended its exploration of her breast, gliding across her stomach to her hip to leisurely knead the soft roundness of her cheek bottom. The skirt of her dress gradually worked its way past her knee to display the beginning curve of her thigh.

Tamara was past the point of resisting anything. It came as a surprise when Bick abruptly broke off the embrace and sat her up in the passenger seat. His hands clasped the steering wheel at the top curve as he lowered his head to conceal it between his arms. Dazed, she watched the deep, shuddering breaths he took to gain control of himself.

"Invite me into the house, Tamara," he ordered thickly. "We'll have dinner. You can do your typing—"

"I would never get past the first 'Whereas the party of the first part,'" she laughed softly at his suggestion. "You would be too much of a distraction, Bick."

"Then don't do the typing." He lifted his head to send her a hotly disturbed look of sheer passion.

"I...can't. I promised Mr. Symington I'd have it done for him and...I need the extra money." Tamara tried to explain.

"Call this Mr. Symington and tell him to find someone else." He dismissed that argument. "If it's the money...how much would you make? Whatever it is, I'll double it."

Tamara recoiled as if he had slapped her. Bick slammed his fist against the steering wheel and cursed savagely. He could have killed himself for making such a blundering remark.

"Tamara, I didn't mean that the way it sounded. I was only trying to tell you that I'd give you the money if you needed it. I'm not poor." He glanced at her wary expression, proud and apprehensive. "No matter what I say you are going to think I'm trying to buy you, aren't you?"

She hesitated. "No...not if that isn't what you meant."

"It isn't." He reached to caress her cheek with the back of his fingers, stroking its curve to the line of her jaw. Her lashes fluttered down. "I know what I went through last night all alone. I don't know if I can take it tonight."

"Bick...there is something I have to tell you," she began.

"No." He pressed his hand against her mouth, restraining the rage that suddenly burgeoned inside him. "I don't want to hear any confessions. I know it's supposed to be good for the soul, but it would play hell with my peace of mind. I know I won't be the first man who has made love to you. I can accept that. But spare me the details. I don't want to know who or when or why!"

She pulled his hand away from her mouth and leaned forward, an earnest frown tracing lines in her forehead. "But I—"

"Do you want proof?" Bick interrupted angrily. "All right, I'll give you proof. Have your dinner and do your typing. I won't interfere because I won't be around. I'll be in my own home going quietly out of my mind. That's what you want, isn't it?"

"Yes. But—"

He sighed and smiled at her wearily. "Then please get out of the car before I change my mind."

She opened the door and hesitated. "Will I sound terribly shameless if I ask whether I'll see you tomorrow?" A smile played with her lips, lips that Bick would have preferred to have against his own.

"I have a board meeting in the morning. It will probably run through lunchtime. They usually do," he said grimly. "But I'll . . . manage to see you sometime tomorrow." The way she was obsessing him, he wouldn't live through the day if he didn't.

Tamara chewed at the inside of her lip as Bick drove away. She had let another opportunity escape her. Turning to the house, she resolved that, no matter what, she would tell him the truth tomorrow. He would understand. To a company the size of Taylor Business Machines, the amount of money she had "borrowed" would be a drop in the bucket. Besides, she was going to pay it back in full and with interest.

Restlessly, Bick prowled the rambling rooms of the large two-story house. The television set was turned on in the informal family room. A stereo was emitting mood music from the four speakers in the rec room. The notes for the morning board meeting were spread out over his desk in the library. A light was on in the kitchen, where the remains of his dinner waited on the countertop for the housekeeper's arrival in the morning.

Pouring a drink from the crystal decanter in the living room, Bick set it down untouched to walk back to the library. He flipped through a Rolodex to the S's and dialed the second number under Slater.

"Hello, Peggy. Bick Rutledge. I'd like to speak to Adam," he requested the instant he received an answer.

"He isn't here. He's working late...or so he told me," was the laughing reply.

"He is?" Bick frowned. "Where? Finishing up the Signet books?"

"That's what he said."

"Did he give you a telephone number?" he asked, since the switchboard would be closed.

"Yes." Peggy Slater gave it to him.

"Thanks." He hung up and dialed the number she had given him. It rang a half dozen times before it was answered. It was Adam's voice on the other end of the line. "Hello, Adam. This is Bick. I called the house and Peggy gave me the number."

"Oh, hello, Bick. What can I do for you?" Recognition replaced the remoteness that had initially been in Adam's voice.

"I want you to transfer Tamara...Miss James to the corporate headquarters. Find her a position on your staff," Bick ordered. There was a long pause. "Adam? Are you there?"

"Yeah, I'm here." He sounded vague, preoccupied, and Bick's gaze narrowed. "I'll find a place for her."

Bick detected a tone he didn't like. "Don't you feel she's qualified?" he challenged.

"Miss James is highly intelligent, skilled, and very knowledgeable." Adam seemed to choose his words with care.

"Then there is no problem," Bick persisted.

"None that I can see at the moment," Adam agreed.

"How come you're working tonight? There isn't any rush in finishing that audit." Adam's attitude troubled him.

"I had some questions. I thought I'd clear them up tonight when I wouldn't have any interruptions."

"Is anything wrong?"

"I don't know," came the sighing answer. "I've got this feeling, but I can't put my finger on it. It's probably nothing."

A smile touched Bick's mouth. Adam was definitely thorough, very definitely a company man.

"Don't stay late. Maybe you'd better give Peggy a call. I think I aroused her suspicions," he joked.

"She's already called me twice. So far I have to bring home a half gallon of milk and a loaf of bread."

A low chuckle rolled from his throat. "Good night, Adam."

"Bick?"

He had started to hang up the phone and stopped at the questioning use of his name. "Yes."

"What's your schedule tomorrow?"

"I have a board meeting in the morning, but I'll probably be free about the middle of the afternoon. Why?"

"No reason," Adam hedged. "I just wondered. Good night."

There was a click on the line. Bick frowned and replaced the receiver. He didn't know what had got into Adam, but he'd probably find out tomorrow when he went over to the office to see Tamara. That stirring ache in his loins returned and he wandered back into the living room to find his drink.

Old man Shavert was droning on. Bick leaned back in his chair at the head of the table and let his pen doodle on the note pad balanced on his knee. He glanced at the words scattered in the margins and a smile twitched at his mouth. A psychiatrist would have a field day interpreting his absent word associations. Profit—tonight. Loss—last night. Liabilities—lack of patience.

The door to the boardroom was opened a discreet crack and a tall, slim elderly woman slipped in and tiptoed to his chair. Mrs. Davies had been his right arm and executive secretary since he had assumed the presidency of the corporation. He knew she would never interrupt a meeting unless she felt it was important. Like a self-conscious schoolboy, he covered his secret references to Tamara on the note pad and turned his swivel chair to listen to her whispered message.

"Adam Slater is on the telephone. He says he isn't going to have another chance to call you this afternoon."

That seemed strange, but Bick was willing to accept any excuse to end the boredom of the meeting. "Excuse me, Gil," he interrupted the man issuing the latest, and longest, in a series of reports. "Let's break for lunch. You can finish your report when we come back."

There was a general nod of approval at his suggestion. Bick didn't wait around to take part in the conversation that broke out, but followed Mrs. Davies out of the room to the privacy of his big office.

"Line two," she told him before closing the door.

"Hello, Adam. What's the problem?" He ripped off the sheet of his note pad and crumpled it into a wad before tossing it in a nearby wastebasket.

"I'd rather not go into it over the phone. Were you planning to stop over here this afternoon?" Adam queried.

"Yes," Bick admitted without actually stating that the purpose of his visit was to see Tamara. "Is something wrong?"

"I'll talk to you about it when you get here." Adam stalled again. "What time do you think it will be?"

Bick frowned and glanced at his slim gold watch. "I shouldn't be any later than three thirty."

"Okay. I'll be waiting for you in Stein's office."

"Stein's office? You are making this all sound very mysterious, Adam," he accused with hesitant amusement.

"I don't mean to, but it isn't something I want to talk about on the phone. It's something you definitely need to know about."

"Does it have anything to do with Ta...Miss James's transfer here?" Bick searched for a reason for his accountant's peculiar secretiveness. "Did you mention it to her?" Had she refused it? He'd wring her neck if she had. My God, he couldn't keep commuting back and forth between his office and hers. He wanted her close so he could have a glimpse of her once in a while, just to reassure himself she existed and wasn't some figment of his imagination.

"No. No, I haven't gotten around to mentioning it to her yet," Adam replied as if he had forgotten all about it.

Bick released a breath of relief. "All right. I'll see you at three thirty... in Stein's office."

"Right."

But it was closer to fifteen till four before Bick walked through the main entrance. He had hoped to be a few minutes early so he could let Tamara know he was in the building, but not by any stretch of the imagination did her office lie on the direct route to that of the former owner's. With an impatient grimace, he continued toward Stein's private office, where Adam was waiting. He nodded curtly to the white-haired secretary sitting at the desk in the outer office.

"Mr. Slater is inside. He's expecting you," she informed him unnecessarily.

"Thank you." Bick opened the door without knocking and walked in. Adam was standing at the window, his back to the door. He turned when Bick entered, a rather drawn and concerned expression on his face. "What's this all about, Adam?" Bick came straight to the point.

Adam hesitated, then did likewise. "There's a discrepancy in the books." He walked from the window to the large desk, where two sets of ledgers were lying open. "There is roughly twenty thousand dollars that can't be accounted for."

"What?" It was a wary, one-word question that didn't really ask for the explanation to be repeated. Bick walked to the desk to study the opened ledgers for himself.

"Now you understand why I didn't want to talk to you about this over the telephone." Adam thrust a hand in his slacks pocket, a certain grimness pulling down the corners of his mouth as he watched Bick. "I had a devil of a time proving to myself it was missing. It's been very skillfully hidden."

There was an icy coldness in the pit of his stomach as Bick followed the penciled notes Adam had made in the columnar margins, tracing the flow of the funds in question. "Who knows about this?" he demanded, fighting the growing feeling of dread.

"Just you and me. Nobody else... except the person who knows where the twenty thousand dollars is." Adam qualified his answer.

"There must be a mistake," Bick stated, groping desperately for an explanation.

"That's what I thought... at first. But there it is—in black and white." Adam gestured toward the account books. "Look for yourself. You can see—"

"Yes! I can see it!" Bick slammed the books shut with sudden violence and turned his back on them. "I can see it but I don't want to believe it!" His hand curled into a tight fist, but there was nothing to strike at. "Maybe there's an explanation," he hoped aloud.

"Do you want me to get Stein in here?" Adam suggested. "Maybe he could clear it up."

Bick released a harsh, laughing breath of scorn. "Don't bother. You know as well as I do that the man probably doesn't know a debit from a credit. He isn't the one who made those entries." Only one person could have—Tamara. He gritted his teeth, a muscle jerking in his cheek at the fierceness of his reaction.

Adam was aware of it, too. There was a long, heavy silence that Bick couldn't break, unable to say what they were both thinking.

"Bick, I'll...uh...talk to Miss James, if you want me to," Adam offered finally.

Bick wanted to push the problem onto Adam's shoulders. The truth was he was afraid of a confrontation with Tamara. He was afraid of what the result might be. Bick tried to rationalize his desire with the thought that Adam would be more objective. But, whatever the outcome, the problem would eventually land on his desk. He had to face it now or be torn apart by questions.

"No, I'll handle it." He forced the words out of his tightly clenched jaw and rubbed a hand over the bands of tension knotting the cords in his neck. "Have...Stein's secretary—whatever her name is— call Miss James and tell her that I want to see her...here."

"Do you...want me to stay or leave the two of you alone?"

"You'd better stay," Bick said, sighing, because he wasn't sure what his reaction was going to be. "At least until we get to the bottom of this."

Chapter Five

Mrs. Danby had said Bick wanted to see her right away, but Tamara didn't need that admonition to hurry down the corridor to Mr. Stein's office. Her stomach was fluttering with nervous excitement. She felt ridiculously like a schoolgirl and sternly reminded herself that she was an adult, not a giddy teenager. But it didn't slow her racing pulse.

Darting a quick smile at the elderly secretary, Tamara walked directly to the door leading into the private office. She knocked once, and a voice that she recognized instantly as Bick's gave permission to enter. Opening the door, Tamara couldn't keep the suppressed joy at seeing him again from sparkling in her jewel-blue eyes. Bick was standing behind Mr. Stein's desk, his attention focused on some papers on its top. Out of the corner of her eye, she caught the movement of a second occupant in the room. She tore her gaze from Bick to identify the second person.

"Hello, Adam." She greeted him naturally and turned back to the man who had summoned her. "You wanted to see me...Mr. Rutledge." She remembered, just in time, to address him formally.

Bick lifted his head and Tamara was frozen by the icy cold look of his green eyes. "Come in, Miss James," he ordered.

As she walked toward the desk, her gaze darted from Bick to Adam to the ledger books on the desk. An alarm bell went off in her head and Bick's next words confirmed what she feared. "Mr. Slater and I want you to tell us what you know about the missing twenty thousand dollars."

"Y...You know about it." Her legs started to turn to jelly.

"Yes." Something savage flickered across Bick's expression.

Unable to stand without support, Tamara slowly lowered herself into the armchair in front of the desk. A faint laugh bubbled from her throat, venting some of her tension.

"I actually feel...relieved that you know about it," she said, a little surprised at that discovery.

Bick appeared unmoved by her admission. "What happened to the money?"

"I borrowed it." Tamara would have followed that statement with an explanation, but she was interrupted by Bick.

"With whose permission?" he snarled, towering behind the desk to physically intimidate her.

There was a puckering frown on her forehead as she tried to defend herself. "With nobody's permission— at least not officially." At the gathering thunder in Bick's features, Tamara hurried on with an explanation so he would understand. "I approached Mr. Stein several times with the intention of asking for the loan," she assured him with a proud tilt to her chin. "But there was always some interruption, or else he was wrapped up in his current project. I needed the money desperately. Since I had borrowed money from him and his brother before, I knew he would loan it to me again. So I took it. I knew he wouldn't mind."

"No, I'll bet he wouldn't," Bick jeered, his strong features cut into harshly contemptuous lines. "When a man is as old as Stein, I imagine he would consider a woman as young and beautiful as you a rare treat and be thoroughly compensated by the 'pleasure' of your company."

"It wasn't like that at all. You make him sound like a lecher," Tamara protested in a stabbing breath. "Mr. Stein has been like an uncle to me. So was his brother before he died."

"Yes, old men tend to adopt beautiful 'nieces,'" he sneered.

Tamara whitened at his vile implication, but before Bick could continue, Adam interrupted, "If it was a loan, then what's the purpose of these entries?"

With difficulty, she forced her wounded gaze to leave Bick to focus on the second man. When she did, Bick walked away from the desk to stand at the window, his legs slightly apart and his hands clasped behind his back. The rigidity of his posture was a clear indication that she hadn't convinced him of her innocence.

"I . . . I was going to put it into the ledger as an outstanding employee loan, but Mr. Stein—the other Mr. Stein, Art, the one who died—had me enter it this way the last time. So I presumed that I should do it the same way with this loan," she explained.

"What kind of trouble are you in, Miss James?" Adam asked gently.

"Trouble?" she repeated blankly. "I'm not in any trouble."

A scornful sound came from Bick. "You are in trouble all the way up to your pretty little neck," he snapped without turning from the window or altering his stance. "When somebody takes twenty thousand dollars, they had better have twenty thousand reasons. So you'd better start telling us yours."

"My mother is . . . terminally ill." Tamara went on to explain the details of the debilitating disease that was killing her mother by inches every day and the constantly increasing financial drain for medical and associated costs of the illness.

"Didn't you have medical insurance?" Adam frowned.

"The bills exceeded the limit the insurance would pay over two years ago. Mr. Stein—Mr. *Art* Stein, that is—loaned me some money shortly after that. I was able to repay it out of the small inheritance my mother received from a distant relative about eight months ago." The last explanation was added for Bick's benefit. "And I fully intend to pay back this loan . . . with interest."

"How?" The one-word taunt came from Bick.

"My mother has a twenty-five-thousand-dollar life insurance policy." Tamara swallowed the lump in her throat and took a firmer hold on her composure. "I know this sounds morbid, but when she . . . passes on, the insurance money will pay the loan. It's only a matter of . . . months." Although she faltered a little, she managed to provide the information without her voice breaking.

"I'm sorry, Miss James." It was Adam who extended the soft words of sympathy.

"That's all, Adam. You may leave," Bick ordered curtly.

After sliding a look at the man rigidly facing the window, Adam smiled thinly at Tamara and left the office. In the silence that followed, Tamara sought Bick's motionless form with a sideways look. It was as if he had turned to stone, hard and implacable and unreachable.

Then the chestnut head was tipped back as he looked up to the blue sky outside the window. "What happens next, Miss James?"

They were alone and he was still addressing her in that polite formality. She felt chilled and rejected. Tamara looked away.

"I don't believe I understand your question," she replied with great dignity, a mask for her hurt.

Bick turned to bring his hard gaze to bear on her. "What is it that you expect me to do?" He rephrased the question into a challenge.

"I expect you to understand."

"Is that all?" A masculine brow was arched to taunt her.

"Yes, that's all," Tamara insisted stiffly.

"Don't you expect me—and Adam—to keep silent about your...'loan?'" He continued to study her over the point of his shoulder.

Confusion clouded her eyes. "I'm sure you'll want to tell Mr. Stein, but I can't think why anyone else needs to know."

"You can't think why?" Bick repeated in an exasperated taunt. "You helped yourself to twenty thousand dollars of company funds and attempted to hide the fact in the ledger entries." Long, impatient strides carried him toward the desk. "That doesn't fall into the category of pilfering. You didn't filch postage stamps. You took twenty thousand dollars!" He emphasized the amount.

"I borrowed it," Tamara corrected.

"That isn't what it looks like," he ground out roughly. "Do you know what it looks like? Embezzlement." Bick flipped open the books and shoved them across the desktop for her to see, but Tamara didn't need to look at them to know what they contained. "You can't expect Adam or myself to keep quiet about this."

"It's only a loan," she repeated, and fought to keep the panic out of her voice with some success.

"Tamara! You aren't dealing with the brothers Stein. This is Taylor Business Machines, a national corporation. I am answerable to stockholders and a board of directors." His voice pounded at her ears. "My actions are governed by federal laws."

"I'm going to pay it back with the insurance money," Tamara reminded him.

"Why the hell didn't you simply cash the policy in?" Bick demanded.

"Because I wouldn't have received even half the face value of it. And that wasn't enough! I don't think you know how much it costs for doctors, a full-time nurse, treatments, and medication, and—" She stopped when she realized she was on the verge of hysteria and didn't continue until she had regained control. "At least I will have the money from the insurance to pay back the loan. That should mean something." She stared at her hands, fingers laced tightly together in her lap.

A weary sigh came from Bick. His head was bent and he was rubbing his forehead, then his eyes, before bringing his hand down over his mouth and chin. The harshness had left the troubled green of his eyes as he picked up a pen and tore off a corner of a message pad.

"Give me the name of your insurance company and the local agent," he requested in a flat, emotionless voice.

Tamara did. "I don't have the policy number with me, but I can get it if you need it." She had always prided herself on being intelligent, but viewing her actions through his eyes, she realized she had acted like a naive idiot.

"I'll let you know if I need it," Bick said without looking at her.

Somehow that made her feel worse than all his insulting insinuations. Unlacing her fingers, she gripped the arms of the chair. "If you don't have any more questions, I'll leave now." When no response was forthcoming, she pushed out of the chair and started for the door.

Before she was three steps away from the chair, a hand was on her arm to spin her around. Then her shoulders were seized in a talon-strong grip and Bick was towering in front of her, dwarfing her with the breadth of his shoulders and searching her face with tortured anger.

"Why? Why, Tamara? Why?" he ground out savagely.

She blinked back the tears shimmering in her eyes and proudly returned his probing gaze. "I have already explained why." She was careful to speak concisely and conceal the tremor in her voice.

A hand slipped from her shoulder to encircle her throat as if he wanted to throttle her for being so incredibly stupid. "I don't think you have any idea how much you have complicated everything," Bick muttered.

In the next second, his mouth was swooping down to cover hers. The leashed violence in his kiss made the possession hard and punitive. He used his mastery to hurt, not to ease Tamara's hurt. The protesting cry she made was smothered by his mouth and her arms came up to push against his chest in resistance.

Her spark of rebellion ignited a counterassault. His arms went around her to encircle Tamara with his male strength and crush her against his chest. The force of it drove the breath from her lungs and Tamara surrendered to her superior foe. In acknowledgment of her submission, the pressure of his mouth subtly changed to a persuasive degree.

The shaping caresses of his hands began to send warm impulses of pleasure along her nerve ends. It started fires that had her lips moving against his in willing response. Tamara melted in his embrace that assuaged all the hurt and banished all the fears. In his virility there was strength; in his strength there was protection.

Her arms were trapped between them, denying each the closeness they sought. Bick loosened his hold and lifted his head, dragging his mouth over her closed eyes to her forehead, his breath warm and moist against her skin. She tried to find a way inside his suit jacket as his hands moved to her waist.

Bending his head again, Bick nuzzled her neck and alternately licked and nipped at her sensitive skin. "Thank God you wore a blouse today," he muttered thickly as his exploring fingers found the front and skillfully freed the buttons from the material.

She heard herself moan softly when his hands slipped inside and dispensed with the front fastener of her brassiere. His mouth moved back to her lips as if to capture the sound. Pulling her with him, Bick moved backward to sit on the edge of the desk. He stretched his legs apart, drawing her in to stand inside.

"I knew your skin would feel like satin," he declared in a husky murmur.

His hands took the weight of her breasts in their palms while his lips began a foray to their slopes. With weakening legs, she leaned against him and curled her hands into the thickness of his hair, pressing his mouth to the crest his tongue teased. The hard outline of his driving need for her was etched against her flesh. Sensations spun round and round in a mindless whirl of desires that preempted coherent thought. There was only now and this moment, when Bick wanted her as deliriously as she wanted him.

A shrill sound tried to break their spell. It made several attempts before Tamara recognized the sound. Bending her head, she brushed her lips against the burning lights in his brown hair.

"The telephone." She identified the sound in case he hadn't.

"To hell with it." Bick denied its importance to lift his head and draw her mouth down to his, but the phone rang shrilly again before their lips more than touched. Tamara sensed his conflict between duty and desire and made the choice for him by drawing away. Bick reached behind him to pick up the receiver. "Yes . . . I did? I'll stop by to pick it up before Mrs. Davies locks the office. . . ."

During the second pause, Tamara became conscious of their surroundings. Although Bick had kept an arm around her hips, she was standing freely. Their passion had carried them both away, but this was neither the time nor the place to make love. Partially returning to her senses, Tamara began refastening her clothes. Bick saw her movement.

"Hold the line." He ordered the party on the other end to wait and pressed the receiver against his chest to muffle their voices. "What are you doing?"

"We'll only be interrupted again," she reasoned.

He drew a deep, shuddering breath and his mouth slanted in a smile of agreement. Removing his arm from around her hips, he lifted his hand to stay her fingers from buttoning the top buttons and leaned forward to kiss the creamy swell of her breast.

With downcast eyes, he moved away from her as if it was an effort to deny himself. The action spoke more volubly than any protest that he didn't really want her to go. When he finally looked at her, Bick had control of himself.

"About your...loan. I'll handle it—somehow," he promised. With a nod of his head, he motioned toward the door. "Now go." Before she could answer him, Bick was raising the receiver again to his ear. Securing the last two buttons, Tamara walked to the door and paused to smooth the front of her blouse and skirt so it wouldn't be quite so obvious what she had been doing.

"Good morning, Mr. Rutledge." The slim, iron-haired secretary greeted him and glanced at her watch.

"Yes, I'm running late this morning, Mrs. Davies," he admitted wryly, and paused at her desk to pick up the day's mail. "You can tell the payroll clerk to dock my check by fifteen minutes."

"You sound testy this morning. And you look like you forgot to go to bed last night," she observed.

"Thanks. You look like a hag this morning yourself," he said, countering her insult. The mirror had told him the same thing when he'd shaved, reflecting the deepening lines in his face.

"Problems?" Mrs. Davies probed with her usual astuteness.

His mouth quirked. "You could say that. Any messages?"

"Yes." She handed him a half dozen slips of paper, which he quickly sifted through.

Bick frowned at the third one. "Who is this Karl Pannell?"

"I believe he said he was an insurance agent. He was returning your call."

"That's right, I did call him." He remembered the name Tamara had given him with a certain grimness. "Did he say when I could reach him?"

"His plans were to be in his office until noon." She supplied the information with her usual efficiency. Bick could tell she was eaten up with curiosity, but he wasn't prepared to satisfy it yet—not until he had settled on his plan of action.

"Thank you." When he saw her gathering the appointment book and note pad to follow him into his office to go over the day's agenda with him, Bick forestalled her. "I have some personal calls to make first, Mrs. Davies. I'll let you know when I'm through."

"Yes, sir." But she plainly wasn't pleased that he was altering their routine.

Her displeasure was the least of his concerns. He left her sitting at her desk with thinly pursed lips and walked into his spacious private office, firmly closing the door behind him. Crossing the thick shag carpeting of autumn rust, Bick set his briefcase on the floor behind the long executive desk and picked up the telephone.

He dialed the number of the insurance company. While the phone rang, he sat down on his chair and unlocked the middle drawer of his desk to take out the employee record card. A receptionist answered and put his call through to Karl Pannell.

"How may I help you, Mr. Rutledge?" the agent inquired after greetings were exchanged.

"A Miss Tamara James has recently joined our employ and we are attempting to straighten out her insurance," Bick lied. "I have been informed that she is named as the sole beneficiary on a life policy issued by your firm for her mother..." He checked the employee record card. "...Mrs. Lucretia James."

"One moment, please, while I check our records," the agent requested.

"Of course." Bick tapped a pen on the desktop while he waited. He wondered if he wouldn't have saved time by simply asking what the insurance company's procedure would be to change the beneficiary to the corporation.

There was a click on the line. "Mr. Rutledge? I'm afraid your information isn't correct."

A stillness came over him. "Do you mean Tamara James isn't the beneficiary?"

"No, the policy is no longer in effect."

His fingers tightened around the telephone receiver, his knuckles turning white. "Since when?" Bick asked carefully, trying to sound only casually interested.

"Let's see. It was cashed in about seven months ago. My notes indicate the insured was in a financial position where the premiums were becoming too much of a burden."

"Seven months ago?" Bick repeated, because he wanted to be very certain about that date. "Are you positive?"

"Yes. I have the record right here in front of me," the man insisted.

"Thank you. I'm sorry I troubled you."

The man made some reply, but Bick was beyond hearing it. Pain was crashing in on his head, shattering his images and destroying his illusions. Numbed fingers dropped the receiver on the hook. There was a burning sensation in his eyes as they began to blur. He had believed her, but she had been deceiving him all along.

"That little liar!" He choked on the words. It hurt to breathe, his chest muscles tightening up in a tortured contraction.

Something exploded inside him, unleashing a torrent of violent energy. He pushed out of his chair and recrossed the room to the outer office. As he slammed the door, the secretary behind the desk turned with a start.

"Cancel all my appointments for today. I don't know what time I'll be back."

It was a growled order that left the woman blinking after him in shock.

After adding the column of figures twice and arriving at the same answer, Tamara entered the total at the bottom of the page. She cleared the adding machine and punched the next number in the following column. The door to her office swung open and she looked up. A smile spread across her features with radiant force as Bick walked in.

"Hello." Her greeting was soft and warm, echoing her feelings. "I didn't expect to see you this morning."

"I'll bet you didn't." His expression was unfathomable, but there was a subdued bite to his voice.

Her gaze ran over the haggard lines stamped into his features. They made him look tougher and harder, and tired. "Sit down. You look like you could use a cup of coffee. How do you like it? Black? Or with cream and sugar?" She stood up, silently volunteering to get him a cup.

"Forget the coffee." But he did sit down in the chair placed in front of her desk.

Tamara was tempted to argue that a cup of coffee would do him good, but the set of his jaw warned her not to do it. So she sat back down and wondered why he hadn't stolen a good morning kiss. Of course, there wasn't anything loverlike in his expression this morning.

"Did you come to watch me work?" Tamara attempted to lighten his apparently black mood.

"No. I want you to repeat what you told Adam and me yesterday." He leaned back in the chair and laid an arm along her desk, picking up a pencil to roll it between his thumb and fingers. The narrowness of his gaze was strangely challenging.

"Again?" A frown flickered across her face.

"Yes. Again."

Tamara hesitated, fighting down a budding apprehension. She began her explanation with an account of her mother's illness and her subsequent financial straits. Bick listened without comment, never taking his eyes off of her. She went into greater detail about her attempts to broach the subject of a loan with Mr. Stein before she took it upon herself to take the money.

"Don't forget the part about the previous loan." Bick prompted her when she paused.

"I...I was just coming to that." The frown became a permanent part of her expression when she continued. She explained the similar position she had been in the previous time and the late Art Stein's offer of a loan. Again Tamara made certain Bick understood she had repaid the loan with money her mother inherited. Lastly, she referred to the insurance policy.

When she finished, Bick set the pencil aside to clap his hands, applauding her with mockery. "Marvelous performance. You did even better than yesterday, but then, you had time to perfect your story, didn't you?" he concluded.

"It isn't a story," Tamara protested in wary anger. "It's the truth."

"I don't think you know the meaning of the word," he jeered. "With a body and a face like yours, you can make a man believe almost anything you want. What were you thinking when you walked out of the office yesterday afternoon? Did you say to yourself, 'The poor, dumb sucker bought every word I said'? How much was I supposed to eventually pay, Miss James? Twenty thousand dollars?''

"What?" She reeled in confusion, staring at him in bewilderment when he stood up to rest his hands on her desk and lean toward her.

"You thought you had hooked yourself a prize fool, didn't you?" Bick accused. "I admit I was—for a while. I thought Adam had made a mistake about the missing funds. I didn't want to believe you had anything to do with it. When you openly admitted that you had 'borrowed' it"—he sarcastically emphasized the verb—"I was enraged. Then you started telling your sad tale. I can't believe I actually swallowed that garbage about your poor, dying mother."

That was too much. Tamara lashed out with her hand, her palm stinging against a hard cheek. The contact sent sharp needles stabbing all the way up her arm. The slap had turned Bick's head at an angle, an ugly red patch rapidly turning white on his suntanned cheek. Moving out of her range, he straightened.

"You made sure I was on your side before you left, too," Bick continued in the same caustic vein. "A little kissing, a little petting, then you left while I was still panting for more. Just for curiosity's sake, how long would it have been before I finally laid you? Had you worked that out on your timetable yet?"

"No!" Tamara was indignant, angry, repelled all at the same time.

"Did you think you were going to get as much out of me as you got out of the Stein brothers? Or were you playing me for bigger game?"

"You're insane." It was the only explanation.

"No." Bick laughed harshly. "I was out of my head for a little while, but not now. You overplayed your hand, Tamara. You are guilty of overconfidence. Before you gave me the name of that insurance man, you should have made certain he was going to play along with you. Or were you just positive that I wouldn't call and check on the policy?"

"Why would I need to talk to him?" she retorted. "If you called him, then you know the details of the policy and its amount."

"You can drop the act now, Tamara." A nerve twitched in his jaw as he looked at her with contempt. "That wide-eyed innocence won't work. There isn't any use pretending anymore."

"It isn't an act!" she flared. "Will you stop saying that!"

"I suppose the next thing you are going to say is that you didn't know the policy was no longer in effect. Or are you suffering from a convenient case of amnesia?" he mocked.

"No longer in effect? You're mistaken," Tamara insisted. "I paid the last premium. There isn't another one due for three more months. I know it hasn't lapsed."

"No, it hasn't lapsed. You cashed it in, remember?" Bick jeered.

"I didn't!"

"Dammit! Quit lying! You cashed it in seven months ago. The agent checked and double-checked the date. When you 'borrowed' those company funds, you knew there wasn't any damned insurance policy to pay them back!'

Tamara breathed in sharply only to have a paralysis grip her lungs. Seven months ago. It couldn't be. It was merely a coincidence that her mother had received the inheritance money seven months ago. There wasn't any connection between the two events.

"The insurance policy doesn't exist," Bick stated after regaining his temper. "And I'm beginning to doubt that your 'sick' mother exists."

"Don't say that," Tamara whispered in choked dismay.

With a long stride, he was at the back of her desk, seizing her wrist and pulling her out of the chair. "Come on."

"Where?" She stumbled after him, pulled by the bone-crushing hold on her wrist. "Where are you taking me?"

"Why, Tamara? Can't you guess?" he mocked. "You are taking me home to introduce me to your dear, precious mother. Unless, of course, she has risen from her deathbed to do some shopping."

With a callous lack of concern, he dragged her out of the office past the members of her staff. He was indifferent to the stares that turned Tamara red with embarrassment. Outside, Bick shoved her into the passenger seat of the car and climbed into the driver's side. Tamara rubbed her wrist, trying to stimulate the flow of blood into her numbed hand and fingers.

They were a block from the office before she ventured to speak. "I think I can explain what happened about the insurance policy."

"Have you had time to come up with a good story?" He ridiculed her maliciously. "You must have an excellent imagination."

Tamara tried to ignore his jibes. "I didn't cash that policy in, but I think my mother did."

"That's good," Bick nodded. "Blame it on your mother. No doubt the two of you are working together anyway."

Tears burned her eyes and she turned her head away from him so he couldn't see them. She stared out the window, her vision blurring.

"I mentioned to you that my mother received a small inheritance about seven or eight months ago," she reminded him in a small voice. "I used most of it to pay back the first loan. At the time that my mother gave me the inheritance check to deposit in the bank, I was so overjoyed at this totally unexpected windfall that I never questioned it."

"You wouldn't want to be accused of looking a gift horse in the mouth, would you?"

Tamara ignored his comment as best she could. "Several times my mother had tried to persuade me to drop the insurance—to cash it in and take what equity it had accumulated because it was becoming so impossible to make the payments. I didn't. Mr. Stein— Art Stein—convinced me the policy was excellent collateral, under the circumstances. So whenever she suggested it, I refused. This last time, I think she took it upon herself to do something about it."

"That's a good try, but not very convincing."

"All right, so there isn't any insurance money—and there won't be!" she was stung into retorting. "But I swear to you I'll pay the money back."

"How?" Bick challenged.

"You can take part of it out of my check every month—make it a regular deduction," Tamara argued.

"My God!" The exclamation was a strangled laugh. "You've got guts suggesting such a thing."

"Why? At least, you are guaranteed you are going to get your money, aren't you?" she flared.

"I presume, of course, that you are suggesting that the deducted payment be somewhere around a hundred dollars a month," he said dryly.

"I will need money to live on," Tamara pointed out.

"Do you have any idea how long it will take to pay back twenty thousand dollars and the interest it would accumulate? Twenty-five years, if you're lucky."

"Yes, I know." She brushed at a tear that slipped from an eyelash. "But I will pay you back."

"Your plan has a flaw."

"What?" she demanded.

"You don't have a job."

"What?"

"You're fired, that's what," Bick retorted.

"Why?" Tamara turned in the seat to give him a stricken look.

"You don't honestly believe that I am going to let you continue working when I have proof that you are a thief!" He sliced her a narrow look. "I wouldn't put you in charge of a petty cash fund, let alone permit you to continue working in an accounting post.''

"But I'm good at my work," she protested.

"Too damned good!" he scoffed. "Adam almost didn't find your little 'loan,' and he's the best. I wouldn't hire you to answer the telephone!"

"But..." Tamara faltered, suddenly panic-stricken. "But I have to work. How can I possibly earn a living?"

"It's a pity you didn't think of that before you got greedy, isn't it?" He slowed the car and turned it into the curb, parking it in front of her house.

Chapter Six

There was a gasp of alarmed surprise when Tamara walked into the house ahead of Bick. It was followed by a relieved "Tamara" as Sadie identified the intruder and pressed a reassuring hand to her fluttering heart. "My land, girl, you gave me a fright walking in like that. What are you doing home?"

"I—" How on earth could she explain? Tamara wondered. So she didn't try. "I'd like you to meet...my employer, Bick Rutledge. This is Sadie Kent, the nurse who looks after my mother."

She saw the sweeping and cynical look Bick made as the two exchanged greetings, a look that appeared to find fault with Sadie because she wasn't wearing a uniform. It had been a mutually agreed decision. Perhaps it was unprofessional, but it kept the house from seeming like a miniature hospital ward.

"How is Mrs. James?" Bick inquired with droll blandness.

Sadie cast a hesitant glance at Tamara before she answered. "I imagine she is overwhelmed with curiosity at this moment to find out what her daughter is doing home in the middle of the morning."

"Then perhaps we should go into her room," Tamara suggested quickly.

"By all means," he agreed.

She was first to enter her mother's room and walked to the hospital bed, bending to kiss her mother's cheek and murmur a greeting. As she turned to face Bick, her hand automatically sought the limp hand of her mother's in an instinctively protective gesture. Her proud look defied Bick to challenge the state of her mother's health.

Making the introductions, Tamara watched his expression, but he showed no reaction—not pity, not doubt, not acceptance—nothing. She wanted to scream at him to admit that her mother was tragically ill and she hadn't been lying. But, of course, she didn't.

"This is a surprise, Mr. Rutledge," her mother said in her concise speech pattern to make her slurring voice more distinct.

"I insisted that your daughter bring me here so I could meet you," Bick stated. "She has told me frequently about you."

"Tamara has mentioned that you have taken her to lunch and given her rides home. She was much too casual about it, I thought, but now I understand why." It was a brightly knowing look she darted to Tamara.

"Mother, please," Tamara murmured, because that remark that had once been very close to the truth was now very far from it.

Her mother made an attempt at an understanding smile and let her gaze return to Bick. "Would you like a cup of coffee, Mr. Rutledge?"

"I would like that, thank you," he said, accepting.

But Tamara was reluctant to leave him alone with her mother. She wavered uncertainly beside the bed, still clutching her mother's hand in a mute attempt at protection.

"I would like very much to talk to you at a greater length, Mr. Rutledge," her mother said with concentrated effort. "But I tire easily. Perhaps it would be better if you drank your coffee in the kitchen with Tamara."

"Of course, Mrs. James." He agreed to that, too. "It has been . . . a pleasure meeting you."

Her mother's eyelids drifted down in a silent acknowledgment of the polite statement before she looked at Tamara to prompt her into movement. Bick waited to follow her out of the front bedroom through the living room to the kitchen. Sadie eyed them curiously as she passed them to check on her patient.

In the kitchen, Tamara walked directly to the cupboard and took two mugs from the shelf. Fresh coffee was in the chrome-plated percolator and she filled the two cups, keeping the mug with the chip in it for herself and handing the other to Bick. Turning her back on him, she walked to the white-painted kitchen table and chairs.

"I suppose you still think it was an act, that my mother was faking it," she accused tightly. "Maybe you'd like to talk to the doctors. I can give you several names to call. One for our family doctor, the specialist's number, his consultant, or maybe—"

"That's enough," Bick snapped. "I am already convinced you were telling the truth about your mother."

"Am I supposed to be grateful?" she challenged, and pulled out a chair to sit at the table.

"You told the truth about your mother, but there's still that matter about the missing twenty thousand dollars," he pointed out in sharp reminder.

And now no insurance money to pay it back—and no job. "Yes, I know." Tamara sighed and cupped both hands around the mug to warm her chilled flesh with its heat. "How am I going to explain this to my mother?" She lifted her gaze to meet his piercing look.

"Tell her you have me wrapped around your little finger. I gave you the day off because I had been making you work so hard," he jeered, letting her see that his opinion of her intention hadn't changed. "I don't know what you're going to tell her. That's your problem."

"What's going to happen next?"

He moved to stand near her chair. "Do you want me to give you the money?"

"Would you?" A wary hope took the dullness from her blue eyes.

Setting his cup on the table, he put a hand on the back of her chair and the other on the table in front of her and leaned down. "Why should I?" Bick challenged.

"Because...you want to help me." Considering the low opinion he held for her, there couldn't be any other reason—not any more. His hard, lean features told her that.

"What would I get out of it?" His hand left the table to curve around her throat and tilt her head back.

Gripped by the throat, she couldn't elude his mouth when it came down to capture hers and force a deeply passionate kiss that flamed her blood. He freed her lips to draw a breath while his hand slid from her throat to possessively cover the roundness of a breast with his palm.

"Lady, you'd be an expensive lay." His insolent comment prompted her into slapping his hand away. The action merely drew a smile as Bick straightened. "And what would it accomplish? It might get you out of trouble for the moment, but inside of a month you'd be badly in need of money again. That probably doesn't concern you, though," he taunted. "With your beauty, charm, and body, you'll find yourself another sucker to supply the cash. That insurance policy is a good ploy. Maybe the next guy won't be smart enough to check on it."

"I didn't deliberately lie about that," she insisted. "I told you I didn't know my mother had cashed it in."

"So you said." His mouth thinned in grim skepticism, and he turned to walk to the door.

Tamara pushed out of her chair. "What are you going to do?"

Bick paused to glance over his shoulder, raking her with his eyes. "That, my sweet, beautiful . . . witch, is something I haven't decided yet. It keeps running through my head that embezzlers invariably wind up in prison." With that, he yanked open the door and walked out of the kitchen, leaving Tamara staring after him in shock.

With the closing of the front door, she collapsed in the chair and buried her head in her hands. What had she done? It had all been so innocent.

"You're back, Mr. Rutledge." Mrs. Davies started to rise from her chair when he entered, reaching for the messages that had arrived in his absence.

Bick swept past her desk. "I don't want to be disturbed—for any reason," he snapped, and was inside his office with the door closed before his secretary could do more than open her mouth.

He walked to the side of the spacious room opposite his desk where the liquor cabinet stood in a corner. It was well stocked, but seldom used. Breaking the seal on a bottle of Scotch, Bick filled a squat glass, bolted down a swallow, and refilled the glass. In a delayed decision, he took the bottle of Scotch with him when he walked to the cream-colored sofa and stripped off his suit jacket and tie. He sat down on the plump cushions and propped his long legs on the coffee table in front of him. With almost single-minded determination, Bick set to work to empty the bottle on the table.

*   *   *

A hand tentatively nudged his shoulder. "Mr. Rutledge?" Mrs. Davies's hesitant voice called his name.

The sound seemed to reverberate on his eardrums and pound through his heavy head. Bick tried to open his eyes and had to cover them with his hand against the sudden glare of light. His mouth felt coated with thick wool and his stomach threatened to revolt if he moved a fraction of an inch.

"I told you I didn't want to be disturbed," he reminded her in a very soft, yet very harsh, voice—but even that jarred him.

"That was yesterday, Mr. Rutledge."

Bick groaned at the misplaced hours.

Another voice, a man's, suggested, "You'd better round up a pot of very black coffee, Mrs. Davies. And some aspirin." Peering through the narrow slit of his lashes, Bick recognized Adam looking down at him with amused sympathy. Mrs. Davies had gone in search of the much-needed remedies. "You really tied one on, didn't you?" Adam observed.

"Hell, I don't remember," Bick muttered.

After three cautiously downed cups of thick black coffee and two aspirin, Bick began to feel part of the human race. He was aware of his sleep-creased clothes and the dark shadow of a day's beard growth on his face.

"More coffee?" Adam suggested.

"Yeah." Bick held out his cup for a refill.

"What's the problem?" Adam asked, settling back in the chair opposite the sofa.

"How to handle Miss James and her twenty-thousand-dollar loan." Leaning forward to rest his elbows on his knees, Bick stared into the black surface of the coffee, the cup held in both hands. "We can't keep the lid on this much longer. I'm going to be forced to take some kind of action, soon."

"That bothers you?"

"Yes. Remember the employee that started a black market business with the company's airline vouchers. The board made sure he got nailed. It's their policy to be tough and come down hard on any employee caught with his hand in the till." Bick rubbed his hand over his face, the stubble rasping across his palm. "They make an example of them so nobody else will get similar ideas."

"In this case, I think you'll agree there are extenuating circumstances," Adam replied. "Plus, there is that insurance policy."

"That's just it." He sighed. "There isn't any insurance policy. She lied about that."

Adam released a whistling breath. "I see what you mean."

"I fired her."

"You had to."

"The part about her mother was true. I went to the house yesterday." Bick took a drink of his coffee, but it seemed to have lost its stimulating effect. The dullness was back pounding at his head. "I shudder when I think about a woman as beautiful as she is spending time in prison for embezzlement."

"It does sound like it was an act of desperation. The courts might take that into consideration and be lenient. She could get off with a suspended sentence and probation."

"What if she doesn't?" He set the cup on the table with a thud and pushed impatiently to his feet.

"I don't suppose there is any way she could raise that much money—a second mortgage on her house or anything like that?"

"The only way she could get her hands on that much money is if I gave it to her." His grimly angry statement brought a long silence. Even without looking at him, Bick knew Adam was thinking he was a prize fool. "That's what she's expecting me to do. The trap is all baited and set, and I've already been nibbling."

"Are you going to?"

"The minute I give her twenty grand, she's going to need more. Which means she's just going to pull the same number on somebody else. She's not only clever; she's lethal. Beauty and treachery, all in one shapely package."

"I think she's just frightened and desperate."

Bick gave Adam a pitying look. He'd believed that, too, for a little while. "I'm sure she is."

"What are you going to do?"

"I'm going to shower, shave, and change clothes." He walked toward the door hidden in a wall mural that led to a private bath and dressing room, complete with a closet containing clean shirts and suits. "After that, I'm going to take care of any urgent business Mrs. Davies has for me. Then I'm going to withdraw twenty thousand dollars from my personal bank account and go visit Miss Tamara James.''

"I thought as much," Adam murmured with a faint smile.

"God knows why I'm doing it," Bick muttered.

It was after two o'clock when he arrived at Tamara's house. The nurse, Sadie Kent, answered his knock. Her expression was pinched with disapproval when she recognized him. She blocked the opening with her tall frame and didn't invite him inside.

"Would you inform Tamara I would like to speak to her for a few minutes?" Bick requested.

"She isn't here."

"Why isn't she? Where did she go?" He snapped out the questions in irritation.

"Ssh, keep your voice down. Mrs. James is resting." The nurse stepped outside and closed the door to glower at him. "She is still under the impression that Tamara is working for you. Tamara doesn't want her mother to know she lost her job until she can find another one."

"Where is she?" Bick repeated.

"Out looking for work."

"In that case, I'll just wait here until she comes home."

The nurse straightened her mouth into a thin line. "Why? Haven't you brought enough trouble to that girl? Large companies like yours are always gobbling up smaller ones and laying people off. It isn't right."

So that was the explanation Tamara had given for losing her job. He might have known she'd come up with a believable story. "I have an offer that I think Tamara will be interested in. May I come inside and wait until she returns?"

"Be quiet, then. Mrs. James is taking her nap and I don't want her to know you're here," the nurse ordered, and opened the door to let him into the house.

When Tamara entered the house a little past three o'clock, Sadie pressed a finger against her lips to indicate her mother was resting and motioned her toward the kitchen. She crossed the room quietly.

"You have a visitor," Sadie whispered.

Tamara pushed open the door and saw Bick seated at the table, a cup of coffee in front of him. "Any luck with our job hunting?"

"Yes." She walked to the counter to pour herself a cup. "I've been hired as a waitress—for more money as a matter of fact. What are you doing here?" His presence was having a rippling effect on her nerves, spreading a fine tension through her system.

"I came to make you an offer."

"What kind of an offer?" Had he reconsidered? Was he going to let her have her job back? Hope flared that maybe not all was lost.

"What would you say if I told you I was willing to give you the twenty thousand dollars to repay your...'loan.'" He hesitated before the last word to underline it.

Tamara sat down, wondering if this was another one of his cruel jokes. "Are you?"

"As long as you agree to the conditions I make."

"Which are?" She scanned his expression, but it was a mask for his thoughts.

"In return for the twenty grand, you will become my wife and—"

"What?"

"You heard me." His mouth slanted, but there wasn't any humor in the suggestion of a smile.

Her pulse was hammering a thousand beats a minute. She hadn't misunderstood. He was proposing, but the green of his eyes held no desirous light. There was no warmth in his look.

"Why would you want to marry me?" she questioned warily.

"For a variety of reasons. I feel guilty about letting you run around loose, yet I can't stand the thought of seeing you in prison," Bick replied, sliding an indifferent look over her face. "And I want you to move into my house and I don't think your mother would approve unless there was a marriage license involved. The license will pacify her and I will pacify you by promising to provide for your mother's comforts and care. I will hire a nurse to live in. You can visit your mother during the day while I work and spend the nights with me when I'm home. Not the least among my reasons for wanting you as my wife is a desire to have some return for my money."

She stared at him. The proposal sounded very cold-blooded in a hot-blooded sort of way. "Do you expect me to agree?"

"I don't think you have any choice." He smiled at her lazily. "Your loan is paid back. Your mother is cared for. You won't have to work. All your troubles are over.''

Or just beginning? "I . . . I don't know.''

"Naturally I will have a marriage contract drawn up, spelling out what you can expect to receive from me. The ceremony can take place a week from Sunday. Since we are just going through the motions for proprieties sake, we'll restrict it to the basics." Bick was talking as if she had already accepted.

"I haven't said I would marry you," she reminded him.

"Considering the alternatives, you aren't going to say no." He leaned back in his chair, draping an arm over the arm-rest. "Unless you have someone else lined up to give you the twenty thousand."

Casting him a hurt and angry glance, Tamara rose from her chair. "No, I don't!" She walked away to stand in front of the kitchen sink, rubbing her elbows in agitation. "I've never tried to line anybody up for anything."

There was the scrape of the chair leg, followed by the sound of his approach. Tamara stiffened at the touch of his hands on her waist, jolted by the electric current that flowed from his fingers. There was a ringing in her ears as his hands moved to the front of her ribs, sliding under her crossed arms, aiming for her breasts. She caught at his wrists to try to stop him while his body heat warmed the length of her backside. His intimate touch ignited tremors that shuddered through her when her weak attempt failed. Then his breath stirred her hair and caressed her ear as he bent his head to lick kisses along the throbbing cord in her neck.

"You've heard my offer," he murmured against her skin. "What more could you want?"

You, she thought. But she would have him if they were married. So why was she hesitating? Exerting only the slightest pressure, Bick turned her around and into his arms. Her breath quickened when his lips traced the outline of hers, his clean male scent inflaming her senses.

"I need an answer," Bick prompted in a low, rumbling voice that disturbed her.

"Yes," Tamara breathed into his mouth, and it stopped tormenting her lips with its feather touch to harden in moist possession.

Its sensual magic had Tamara straining toward him and his hands moved to aid in her progress, pressing her fully to his virile length. She stopped thinking altogether about his unemotional proposal and concentrated on feeling the unmistakable and passionate hunger in his embrace, a consuming fire that ran just as deep and hot within her.

The pressure of his mouth was already easing from her lips when the door opened and Sadie walked into the kitchen. "Oops!" She turned to leave.

"Don't run off, Ms. Kent," Bick instructed in a low drawl, lifting his head to glance at the nurse. "Congratulations are in order. Tamara has agreed to marry me."

"She has? Do you mean that was your offer?" Without waiting for his answer, her gaze raced to the kiss-softened features of Tamara's face, all signs of tension and stress gone. "That's wonderful."

Incapable of saying anything, Tamara remained within the circle of his arms, leaning against him. When she sensed his eyes on her, she lifted her head. The hardness was back in his look, chips of green stone regarding her.

"Yes, it is wonderful," Bick agreed, but the dryness of his voice was searing.

"Your mother is going to be so happy when you tell her," Sadie declared in a watery voice. "She's awake now."

His encircling arms were withdrawn, leaving Tamara momentarily bereft, until her hand was engulfed in the largeness of his. "We'll go tell her the news."

Her mother took the announcement calmly, although she expressed concern at their haste when she learned the wedding was a little more than a week away. Bick smoothly reassured her that neither he nor Tamara were rushing into it. With skillful tact, he conveyed the impression that the marriage was taking place so soon because of her failing health and Tamara's wish to have her mother present at the occasion.

When he was through, her mother was convinced of the rightness of their decision. By implication, he made it clear that Tamara would no longer be working, saying he would arrange to have her job filled immediately so she would have the week before the wedding free. Under his persuasive charm, her mother's apprehensions appeared groundless without

Tamara needing to add her assurances. In fact, she had taken very little part in the conversation.

Barely twenty minutes later, she was walking him to the door so he could return to his office. She was a bit dazed to realize that their engagement was an accomplished fact, unquestioned by anyone. She raised no objection when Bick drew her outside the door as if he wanted to say his goodbye to her in private, and beyond the benevolent curiosity of the nurse.

"Now that we have that settled," he said when the door was closed and they couldn't be overheard, "we have a couple more details to get straight." He was all very businesslike again, organized and aloof. "I won't be physically giving you the money. I will simply repay the . . . loan in your behalf."

His statement implied a lack of trust and Tamara was stung into replying, "Do you think I would spend it on something else?"

"I don't intend to find out," Bick said, smiling coldly. "The other matter is a ring. What size do you wear?"

"Five. And I'm not allergic to jewelry," she added. "I had sold what I had and used that as an excuse as to why I didn't wear any."

"Is that information a veiled suggestion to buy you something expensive?" he taunted. "Do you think you might want to sell it someday?"

"No to both questions," Tamara retorted, but Bick seemed unimpressed by her abrupt denial.

"Don't forget to call the restaurant and tell them you aren't hiring on as a waitress." He shifted the subject easily.

"I won't." There was a moment of hesitation as she realized all that he was doing for her and the way he had eased her mother's mind. "I am grateful for what you're doing." Her words were stiff and tentative.

He laid his fingers along her jaw, lifting it fractionally to let his gaze skim her face. "A week from Sunday, you can show me just how grateful you are."

Tamara quivered at the primitive message in his look. A smile slashed at his mouth before his hand fell away and he was turning to walk away.

Chapter Seven

"You may kiss the bride," the minister prompted with a smiling look.

Tamara's hand trembled in the firm clasp of Bick's, the gold band cold on her finger, as she hesitantly turned to face him. The possessive look in his eyes brought the color back to her face, erasing the chill to warm her blood. His mouth descended to fuse itself to hers in a kiss that forever stamped his ownership.

When he released her, it took Tamara a full minute to assimilate her surroundings. Bick's arm was around her waist in support as they stood near the foot of her mother's bed, accepting the minister's congratulations. Then Sadie, who had been one of the witnesses, was giving her a teary hug and admonishing Bick to be good to Tamara. After that, Adam bent to brush a kiss across her cheek and shake hands with

Bick while his wife, Peggy, offered them both her best wishes.

Her gaze sought the figure in the hospital bed, the only other remaining person to observe the ceremony, a wedding performed with only the essential ingredients: no baskets of flowers, no wedding party, no tiers of candles, no white wedding dress. A small cake and a bottle of champagne to toast the happy couple were waiting in the living room. Her mother's expression radiated her inner happiness and contentment. To Tamara, it made up for the brutally cold marriage contract she had signed that disavowed any personal claim to Bick's fortune, granted her nothing but her personal possessions in the event of a divorce, and stated his intention to care for her mother as long as she lived. She had objected to nothing contained in the document, but it carried its own sense of foreboding because it spoke volumes of Bick's lack of trust.

"Happy, darling?"

Bick's use of an endearment startled Tamara, but the sharpness of his gaze said she was frowning. Instantly she smoothed the expression away and smiled with forced gladness.

"Is there a reason why I shouldn't be?" she countered. At the sudden clenching of a muscle in his jaw, she changed the subject. "I think Mother would like to congratulate us."

"Of course." The pressure of his hand on her waist guided her to the side of the bed where Tamara bent to kiss the flaccid cheek of her mother.

"You make a beautiful bride, Tamara." Her mother beamed and glanced at Bick. "Make her happy. She deserves to be."

"I promise you, Mother James, that I will do everything I can to make certain Tamara receives all that she deserves," he replied, and Tamara was the only one who heard the alternate meaning in his vow.

"Time to cut the cake." Sadie wheeled the trolley cart into the bedroom so Lucretia James could observe the wedding ritual.

Leaving her mother's bedside, Tamara was escorted by Bick to the cart. The flat cake was inscribed with their names and decorated with ribbons and rosettes of frosting. Tamara's hand shook slightly as she held the cake knife with its lace bow on the handle and cut the first slice. The flashbulb on Sadie's camera went off when Tamara raised the piece of cake to Bick's mouth and watched him take the bite.

Then it was her turn. She was nervously conscious of the tanned fingers offering the cake to her and the intensity of his watching gaze. Her attempt at a small bite resulted in a smear of thick, creamy frosting coating her lips. The cake tasted dry when she swallowed it hastily in order to lick the excess frosting from her lips. She couldn't get it all and reached for a napkin stamped with silver wedding bells.

She never got the napkin to her mouth as Bick's hand closed around her wrist to stop her. "No." The soft word was followed by a gentle tug that brought her close.

Turning her slightly to block her from the view of the few wedding guests, he lowered his head and opened his mouth on her lips, his tongue darting out to lick away the frosting with infinitely thorough care. The pure sensuality of his action drew a sighing moan from her throat. She could taste the sweetness of melting frosting, unsure whether it came from his tongue or her own.

The minister coughed delicately and Bick pulled away, breathing in deeply for control. Scarlet flames stained Tamara's cheeks, the embarrassed flush spreading down her neck.

"I'll cut the rest of the cake now," Sadie volunteered, stepping forward to pick up the knife. "Would you want to take a slice to your mother?"

"Yes." Tamara seized the chance to escape the man whose caress nearly robbed her of any feeling of shame. It was unnerving to be infected with such wantonness, even if he was her husband.

Bick didn't attempt to keep her at his side when she took the china dessert plate with its wedding cake and silverware to her mother's bed. Aware that his eyes followed her, she sat on the edge of the bed to feed her mother the cake.

"You do love him very much, don't you?" her mother stated.

Tamara didn't argue. "Is it so obvious?" she said instead. Her mother's sigh was a long, sad sound that made Tamara study her with anxious eyes. "What's the matter, Mama?"

"I am happy, but"—she hesitated on the qualifying word—"but I just realized that I won't live long enough to see my grandchildren."

Tamara couldn't smother the audible gasp as a rush of tears burned her eyes. "Oh, Mama." She bit at her lip.

"Please don't cry," her mother scolded. "I am truly happy. There was a time when I thought I would never meet the man you would marry. I feel very lucky. You can't know how relieved I am that you won't be shouldering all this responsibility on your own any-more. There is someone to care for you now."

"Someone to look after both of us," Tamara cor-rected.

"Yes, that's true. And don't you go rushing and try to have a baby right away because of what I said," her mother added.

"I won't. Besides, Bick doesn't want children right away." She thought that was a safe guess, consider-ing his apparent lack of trust in her.

"That is wise. It's good to have time together first."

Pop! The champagne cork sailed into the air. Tamara turned to look as Bick let the foam from the sparkling wine bubble into the first of a row of glasses.

"Set the cake on the bedside table and go drink your toast," her mother ordered.

By the time Tamara had set the plate on the table and risen from the bed, Bick had crossed the room to bring her glass. The toast was a simple wish for their happiness, offered by Adam, but Tamara wondered afterward if the wish was truly simple.

Very soon the conversation began to lag. Bick glanced at her mother. "I believe the excitement is beginning to tire you, Mother James. It's time we left."

"Yes, I suppose it is," she agreed so concisely. "Your honeymoon is going to be very short. You will want to enjoy every minute of it."

Bick swirled the remaining champagne in his glass with absent concentration. "Yes, we will. Unfortunately, the bridegroom has to go to work in the morning." He drained the glass and tossed Tamara a veiled look. "But I think my bride would have been homesick for her mother if we had taken a trip."

"We have been very close," her mother said.

"We will always be," Tamara promised.

The goodbyes began and a reissuance of congratulations. The ever-romantic Sadie even managed to shower them with a handful of rice as they walked out the door. As Bick helped her into the car, Tamara's gaze was drawn back to the house. Even though Sadie had given up her apartment and moved in to be with her mother at night, she felt tugged in two directions. Despite her half-formed anxiety toward her marriage, Tamara couldn't deny she was excited by the man who was her husband, but the feeling of responsibility for her mother was equally strong. Bick noticed the direction of her gaze and flicked a backward glance at the house.

"I wonder if your mother knows the lengths you are willing to go for her," he mused with faint cynicism.

The comment was one that went over and over in her mind during the drive to his house. How much of her decision to marry was because of her mother and their resulting financial dilemma? Tamara realized that she wouldn't have accepted this proposition from just any man. Her attraction to Bick Rutledge was volatile and strong, bordering on love. She had to admit that her acceptance was due, in no small measure, to the man who had asked her.

Bick stopped the car in a cul-de-sac culminating in front of a brick, pillared mansion in a plush, residential area. Its size was awesome compared to the home she had known much of her life. Tamara felt the intimidation of its subdued grandeur as she followed Bick to the white double doors of the front entrance. Unconsciously she edged closer to him.

As he unlocked the door, her gaze ran over the expensive blue material of his suit, cut to frame the broadness of his shoulders and tapering to the muscled slimness of his waist and hips. The sun glinted on his hair and bronzed the angled planes and hollows of his face. A grain of rice had become caught in the notch of his lapel. Her reaction was instinctive as she reached out to brush it away. At her touch, Bick turned his head sharply.

"Sadie's rice," she explained.

Continuing to hold her gaze, he pushed the door inward, then smoothly scooped her into his arms to carry her over the threshold. For a fleeting moment, held close to him with her arms around his neck, Tamara actually felt like a bride. Once inside the large foyer, he set her down.

The ceiling was all the way at the top of the second floor and a Y-shaped staircase opened onto the foyer, white wrought-iron railings curving to the base, where large black squares of tile alternated with white. Tamara looked around, feeling lost.

"Come," Bick said, observing her expression and taking her hand. "I'll give you a quick tour of the house. We won't bother with the second floor." He dismissed the staircase with a glance. "It's where the guest bedrooms are." He led her through an arched opening. "This is the formal living room. Through here is the family room." His whirlwind tour was permitting her only a glimpse of each room, his hand pulling her on without giving her a chance to linger. "At the end of this hallway is the rec room, with a pool table, stereo, et cetera." He opened a door for her to look in. "This is my study." She glimpsed a wall of books, a desk, fireplace, and matching sofa and armchairs before he began to partially retrace their steps. "This is the dining room. Beyond that door is the kitchen. Downstairs is a sauna and exercise equipment. There's a swimming pool in the backyard, too."

"And you live here all alone?" Tamara remarked incredulously. A dozen people could live in the house without being on top of each other, she thought, as he led her down another hall.

"No." He paused, his hand resting on a doorknob, and skimmed her face. "*We* live here all alone." He pushed the door open and drew her inside, letting her step in front of him and bringing his hands up to rest on the top of her shoulders near her neck. "And this is the master bedroom."

It was larger than the living room in her own home, dominated by a queen-sized bed covered with a chocolate brown satin in contrast to the cream carpeting on the floor. A small divan and armchair occupied a corner, upholstered in complementing colors.

"Your clothes are in that closet and the drawers of that dresser," Bick pointed, referring to the majority of her clothes that she had packed and sent with him the previous day. "That door leads to a dressing room and private bath with a sunken tub."

Her gaze was drawn back to the bed. She was intensely conscious of his thumbs absently stroking the nape of her neck, making lazy circles that sent out sensual ripples undulating over her skin. She was caught by a yearning so strong, it was almost physical.

"Are you hungry?" Bick inquired, his head bending slightly to enter her side vision.

"Not particularly," Tamara admitted, since the craving that was making her feel weak had nothing to do with food.

"Good." One hand slid part way down the bareness of her spine and then Bick let his mouth take its place.

Drawing a breath in a soundless gasp, she felt the heat waves radiating through her body. The slow, silent release of the back zipper of her dress had her stomach tightening in delighted shock. As the material loosened around her bodice and waist, his hands moved to adeptly slide the dress from her shoulders and off her arms. The dress rustled into a soft heap about her feet and she was being turned around by hands that had returned to her shoulders.

The eagerness she felt seemed improper. She tried to conceal it as her gaze slowly worked its way past his buttoned shirt front to the knot of his tie and the tanned column of his throat. The firmly defined curves of his mouth were nearly her undoing, her attention lingering on them for a few heart-pounding seconds. Then her gaze traveled the last few inches to his eyes, dark green and burning into her with the impatience of his desire.

They blazed in dissatisfaction over the lace cups of her silk slip that concealed the swelling ripeness of her breasts from his view. When his critically inspecting gaze returned to her face, it swept over the silver-gold frame of her hair, drawn back in its sophisticated knot. Her heart was hammering so loudly, Tamara was certain he could hear it.

"Will you take your hair down for me?"

With a bobbing nod, Tamara agreed and wondered how Bick could speak so calmly when she was being rocked by the passionate upheaval going on inside her. His hands released her and she was free to move. It was a revelation to discover she could walk and the floor beneath her feet was actually solid.

Moving to the dresser and its large vanity mirror, she raised her hands to the back of her head to begin pulling out the pins that held her lustrous blond hair in place. Her fingers fumbled in their initial attempt before the first hairpin was deposited on the dresser top.

Bick watched her every move in the mirror with disconcerting interest. Tamara could see his reflection, too. Her pulse accelerated when he reached up to loosen the knot of his tie. Without taking his eyes away from her reflection, he pulled off the tie and shrugged indifferently out of his suit jacket. Tugging his shirt free from the waistband of his trousers, he began unbuttoning it.

When it had joined the jacket and tie on a chair seat, her hair was tumbling loose about her shoulders. Unconsciously Tamara was inhaling deep drafts of air, disturbed by the naked male torso joining her reflection in the mirror. Sun-bronzed skin was stretched tautly across bunched and sinewy muscles, broken only by a curling cloud of chest hairs.

Assailed by his potent masculinity, she fell victim to a feeling of inadequacy. Dropping her gaze, Tamara reached for the hairbrush on the dresser and began running the bristles through the length of her pale silk hair. Although she wasn't looking at him, her peripheral vision saw Bick move to her side. Her brush stopped in midstroke when she felt his fingers on her hair, catching thick strands to inspect them. Tamara lifted her gaze to the mirror to find him studying her reflection.

"I knew you would look like this with your hair down." There was that calmness of his voice again, so at odds with the ravishing message in his eyes. "Don't wear it skinned away from your face anymore. Let it fall loose around your neck and shoulders."

At this moment Tamara would have walked through fire if he had ordered it. Not trusting her voice, she inclined her head in silent agreement. The action freed the strand of hair from his fingers and Bick moved away. Her gaze followed him in the mirror. She was self-conscious about the excitement that raced through her veins when he paused beside the bed to strip back the covers.

Setting the brush down, Tamara reached under her slip to remove her panty hose while he wasn't looking, not wanting him to see how shamelessly eager she was to have him make love to her. But when she straightened, she discovered he had been watching her. It triggered nervous tremors that rippled out from the core of the quake that had started in her midsection.

"Do you think my haste to get you in bed is indecent?" Bick slowly began to cross the room to the dresser where she stood.

She wished he would smile to ease the tension that was tying her in knots because of his frankly sexual look. They were man and wife. This was their wedding night. The course of events was perfectly natural, yet the anticipation was so intense she ached.

Bick was standing in front of her before Tamara managed to get out an answer. "No." Barely audible.

His hands moved to her ribs, gathering the material of her slip into folds and slipping it over her head. Her skin shivered in a sudden chill, but it was instantly warmed by the touch of his hands encircling her to unfasten the clasp of her bra and remove it, too. Tamara struggled to lift her gaze from the bareness of his chest. In the end his hands cupped her face to help her. The smoldering arousal that she saw in his eyes made her bones melt.

"Before I'm through, I'm going to know everything about you," Bick declared under his breath. "Every intimate detail."

A tiny sound came from her throat at the heady promise. It was the catalyst that unleashed his checked desire. As his kiss bruised her lips, his arms gathered her close. Tamara wound her arms around his middle to cling to him and caress the flexed muscles of his broad back. Their body heats combined in a fusion of bare skin, broken by the waistband of his trousers digging into her stomach.

Bending her backward, he shifted an arm downward to curve it across the back of her thighs and pick her up. His mouth didn't cease its ravishment of her lips as he carried her to the bed he had readied for them. He paused to shed the last barrier, but the satin sheets didn't have a chance to cool her bare flesh before he was stretching his length on the mattress beside her and covering her lips once more.

The pillow was withdrawn from beneath her head and Tamara was drowning in a sea of sensations, caught in a powerful undertow that gave her glimpses of heaven. His caressing hands and seeking mouth fathomed out the mysteries of her flesh until all the sensitive and vulnerable areas had been explored. Urged and aroused by his expert knowledge of the art, Tamara begged him with her lips, her hands, and her body to make love to her and end this feverish ache. Bick let her writhe and twist for a few minutes more before the cloud of dark chest hairs settled over her feminine peaks.

Bick lay on his side, the satin pillowcase cool against his cheek. Morning sunlight streamed over his shoulder to shine on the face of the woman lying beside him. Serene contentment was etched in her sleeping expression, her beauty pure and wholesomely earthy.

The bedcovers were down around her waist, but it was her face that Bick studied. She looked so open, so guileless, this enchantress in the guise of a woman who had trapped him in her spell. By possessing her body, Bick had thought to end his obsessive need for her. But having her once had only strengthened her hold on him. It had angered him into taking her a second time.

Then, in the night, he remembered waking, surprised and delighted to find a womanly shape nestled against him. But he wasn't contented for long to have her merely lying along his side and he had kissed her awake to arouse the desire he knew lurked just below the surface.

The impulse was growing to do it again. Bick leaned toward the lips that were softly parted as if in unconscious anticipation of his action. He thought of the many things he had whispered to her when they had made love. A surge of male pride gave him the strength to resist the temptation of her lips.

She shifted slightly in sleep, turning from him and thrusting her breasts into the air. A swelling heat stirred in his loins and Bick rolled away to sit up on the side of the bed before the tide of lust overwhelmed his self-control.

Self-disgust filled him as he pushed from the bed and stalked to the bathroom. Bick ignored the luxury of the sunken tub for the punishing sting of a cold shower. Why had he bothered to marry her? Why hadn't he simply installed her in this house as his mistress? What kind of a man was he to fall in love with a lying thief? A war raged in his mind as he tried to make excuses for what she'd done. The arguments for her guilt and innocence were equally balanced. The deciding factor was whether he believed her unsubstantiated story or the damning evidence. And Bick didn't trust his feelings. They were too strongly influenced by his romantic attachment for her.

When Bick emerged from the bathroom, Tamara was still sleeping. He paused beside the bed, drawn again by the allure of her half-covered body. With a sharp pivot, he walked to his chest of drawers and pulled out clean clôthes.

The aroma of freshly perked coffee and bacon frying drifted into the room as Bick was smoothing his tie under the collar of his shirt. He glanced at his watch. Freyda Grimes, his housekeeper and cook, was right on time. Standing in front of the mirror to knot his tie, his gaze caught a movement reflected in the mirror. Tamara was waking. For a half second he froze as he watched her looking for him. The instant she saw him, he quickly busied himself with the tie.

"Why didn't you wake me?" she accused softly and slipped out of bed to put on the robe lying at the foot of the bed.

"There wasn't any need." Bick steeled himself not to be swayed by the tenderness in her expression.

"What kind of wife would I be if I let my husband go to the office without any coffee or breakfast?" She sent him a laughing yet intimate glance.

"I have a housekeeper who does that so I don't require your services in that area," he told her bluntly. His cold gaze flicked briefly to her reflection in the mirror in time to see the shock register in her expression.

"But I'm your wife." There was a faint pause. "Aren't I?"

"I gave you my name and you share my bed." He finished knotting the tie and smoothed the ends down his shirt front before buttoning his suit jacket.

"And that's all?" It was a quiet challenge. "Aren't I entitled to anything else?"

Such as what? His love? His trust? His pride? His self-respect? Bick turned away from the mirror and her still reflection, avoiding contact. "You are entitled to what I give you, as our marriage contract states, and nothing more." She had the look of a wounded animal, but he would not allow himself to relent. "Excuse me. My breakfast is ready." Bick left the room before he started listening to his heart.

Chapter Eight

Lightning crashed and the ground trembled with the rumbling thunder that followed. The rain was coming down in sheets, whipped by a strong wind. Caught without an umbrella, Tamara was drenched to the skin by the violent July storm that had unleashed its fury shortly after she had left her mother's house. Her only protection against the downpour was the plastic rain cap she carried in her purse. Her hair was the only part of her that was dry when she entered the front doors of the brick home.

Freyda, the housekeeper, was in the foyer within seconds after Tamara had entered, down on her hands and knees wiping up the puddles of water Tamara was leaving on the polished floor. Tamara heard the woman muttering in ill temper, as if she had deliberately got caught in the storm so she could track the floor. She made a face at the crouched figure and hurried to the master bedroom to take off the wet clothes.

Before she started to undress, she turned on the water to fill the sunken tub and added a heaping portion of bubble bath. By the time her wet clothes were hung up and dripping noisily on the tiled floor, the tub was more than half full. Tamara had barely submerged up to her neck in bubbles when the bedroom door was opened and she heard Bick demanding, "Tamara?"

"I'm in here!" she called, raising her voice so it would carry through the closed door of the bath.

She glanced up when it burst open. His eyes contained that hard gleam she had come to expect after these first weeks of their marriage. The promise of happiness she had found that first night had never materialized, although every time she was in Bick's arms she kept seeing glimpses of it again.

"What are you doing taking a bath now?" he demanded impatiently. "Don't you know storm warnings have been posted?"

"I guessed as much," Tamara admitted and soaped a leg. "This is one of the safest places in the house—solid walls, no windows. And I wanted a warm bath after my drenching coming home from Mother's."

That was where she spent every day. Initially she had attempted to do her part of the housework and cooking, but Freyda had regarded her help as interference and complained to Bick. He had immediately sided with the housekeeper.

"Get out of there and get dressed," he ordered, and grabbed a long bath towel from the rack.

Defiance flared briefly in her blue eyes before she quelled the spark of rebellion to mount the steps leading out of the sunken tub. At the edge, she paused to rinse the bubbles off her legs.

"Hurry up!" Bick snapped and held out the towel.

"Why don't you bring it over here? Or are you afraid of getting your suit wet?" Tamara challenged, and flicked the water from her fingers in his direction.

She realized that she was being deliberately provocative, trying to entice him into making love to her. At least when he held her, he made her feel good. In his arms, she didn't hear words that cut. She could see he wasn't indifferent to her nudity, but he was fighting it.

With a quick toss, he hurled the towel at her. "Get dried off and get some clothes on." Turning on his heel, he walked out of the bathroom.

Tamara clutched the towel, her head dipping down in mute defeat. A few painful seconds passed before she began wiping the moisture from her skin. Her robe was hanging on the door. She wrapped it around her and tied the sash.

When she entered their bedroom, she avoided looking at him and walked straight to her vanity table, where a bottle of moisture cream sat. He had changed out of his suit into a pair of slacks and a casual shirt in a striped knit. Sitting in front of the mirror, Tamara began smoothing the cream onto her face and neck.

"Why are you wearing your hair like that? I told you I didn't like it," he said curtly.

Tamara let her gaze meet his disapproving reflection in the mirror and managed a stiff but calm reply. "I didn't want to get it wet while I was taking a bath." She removed the three hairpins that had held it in a loose coil and recapped the bottle of moisturizer.

"I was informed today that I have abused the privilege of a newlywed long enough and it's time we began accepting invitations," Bick stated in a faintly cynical tone. "We have been invited to a dinner party Friday night by Gil Shavert, one of the directors on the board. I accepted."

Tamara's response was instant and instinctive. "I don't have anything to wear." In the years when she worked and took care of her mother, there had been no demand for gowns or cocktail dresses. It was certain that the invitation would require such an item.

"I don't know why I'm surprised to hear that. I should have expected it, shouldn't I?" The dryness in his voice was taunting. "I suppose now you want to open an account in your name at some exclusive dress shop where you can charge to your heart's content."

"I suppose you think I'm making it up." Her lips thinned into a tight line of suppressed anger.

She didn't wait for an answer, but walked to her closet. With a jerking movement, she stripped the hangers of dresses from the pole and carried them back into the bedroom. She began showing them to Bick one by one.

"Perhaps I should wear this one, or this one, or this one." As each dress was shown, she tossed it on the bed, piling them one on top of the other. The last one happened to be the ivory dress she had been married in. "Or maybe I can wear my wedding dress," she challenged.

"You could," Bick agreed smoothly.

Tamara caught back the sob before it escaped her throat. "Then that's what I'll do." She gathered the dress to her waist and carried it back to the walk-in closet. For an extra minute she stayed there, opening her eyes wide and staring at the ceiling to hold the tears at bay.

He was always doubting her, mistrusting her, questioning her motives. She understood that it all went back to the loan and the insurance policy and his continuing doubt that she had told him the truth. He had rescued her, but not because he believed her. It was always a tangible thing between them, except when they made love. That was when Bick praised her, told her the way she made him feel, the way she affected him. She told herself that she had to be patient and wait. Eventually he would see that she had told him the truth, because she knew he cared. Knowing that, she could hold on and take these moments.

Friday afternoon Bick was already home when Tamara returned from the daily visit with her mother. She could hear the shower running in the master bath. A lavender chiffon dress was carefully arranged on the bed, complete with a matching sheer shawl and a pair of silver heels and evening bag. Her fingertips touched the material while her gaze ran hesitantly toward the closed bathroom door. Her expression softened.

But when Bick came out a few minutes later, Tamara didn't mention the dress and neither did he.

Tamara wasn't sure if he had bought it for her because he wanted to apologize for his unfair accusation or because he didn't want to be embarrassed by having her wear a dress that wasn't proper for the occasion. Since he didn't volunteer his reason, she wouldn't ask. She was also entitled to pride.

The lavender dress was a stunning creation that complemented her fair looks and gave her an immeasurable boost of confidence. But her stomach was churning nervously when Bick parked the car along the circle drive of a large, white house. The guests would be associates of Bick's and she desperately wanted to make a good impression.

"Can't you smile?" he growled under his breath, and helped her out of the car. Tamara realized that apprehension had been tearing at her expression and tried to relax. Bick didn't appear satisfied by the attempt as he took her arm to walk to the front entrance. "You are my wife with whom I have fallen madly in love. Try to remember that and act the part." His sarcastic tone made a mockery of the words. "Acting is something you do very well, isn't it?"

"You keep telling me I do," she murmured.

His attitude made it a chilling beginning, but his attentiveness in the company of their host and his guests soon warmed her. His looks were gentle and loving as Bick rarely left her side. He seemed to find excuses to touch her. Before the evening was over, Tamara couldn't have cared less what the others thought about her. The evening with Bick had shown her what it could be like between them.

The circumstances that had led up to that evening prompted Tamara to make a decision. Her personal checking account was down to a few dollars—what remained of her last paycheck. Since Freyda Grimes did all the household shopping, the only money she had needed before was for bus fare back and forth to her mother's and a few personal items. She was too stubborn to ask Bick for spending money and invite another one of his veiled insults.

There was an obvious alternative of working to earn her own money. It was a simple matter to contact the variety of clients for whom she had done typing in the past. Her typewriter was still at her mother's house. Since her mother was resting much of the time, Tamara could spend a few hours typing during her visits. It gave her the little bit of cash she needed, as well as giving her a feeling of independence.

Tucking the box of addressed envelopes more firmly under her arm, Tamara glanced briefly around the hotel lobby before walking to the desk. A clerk directed her down a hallway to the office of the convention and tour planner.

"You finished them!" was the delighted exclamation from the girl behind the desk. "You don't know what a relief that is."

"I'm sorry I'm a few minutes later than I said I would be when I talked to you earlier," Tamara offered in apology as she set the box of envelopes on the girl's desk. "The bus was running behind schedule."

"It's all right. We appreciate getting these so quickly and that you were able to deliver them."

"It wasn't very far out of my way," she assured her. "The invoice is inside the box."

"Here, let me pay you." Lifting the box lid, the girl read the invoice and unlocked the petty cash drawer, counting out the exact amount into Tamara's hand.

"Thanks." With a quick glance at her watch, she said, "If you need some more typing done, please call me. I'd better go before I miss my bus home."

"Thanks again," the girl called after her.

Tamara retraced her route along the corridor to the lobby. Her destination was the bus stop on the street corner outside the hotel.

Bick listened attentively to the pedantic voice of the German business representative, but his gaze wandered about the lobby. Almost absently he noticed the blond woman entering the lobby from a side corridor, thinking to himself that her hair was almost the same color as Tamara's. Realization flashed that it was Tamara. His pulse leaped and her name hovered on his lips. Before he could call out to her, jealousy closed his mouth with a bilious taste. She was supposed to be visiting her mother, so what was she doing in the hotel? Where had she been coming from? There were no restaurants or lounges down that corridor—only hotel rooms and meeting rooms. Rage billowed within him, ugly and cold. His temper wasn't improved by the presence of his German companion. It prevented him from going after Tamara.

Tamara saw the day's mail sitting on the living room coffee table, but she didn't bother to look at it. There wouldn't be anything for her anyway. Picking up a magazine, she leaned back on the flowered sofa and leafed through it without interest. It had been pointless to return to her mother's. She would have been able to stay less than forty minutes before catching her bus here. But what was she going to do with herself now?

The housekeeper, Freyda, wouldn't welcome her help in the kitchen or anywhere else. The woman seemed averse to company, never wanting to exchange idle chitchat or discuss even the most trivial thing. Tamara sighed, and the sound seemed to echo through the large, empty house.

When the front door opened, Tamara looked over the back cushion of the sofa. Her smile of welcome was spontaneous and glowing.

"Hello. You're home a little early today," she greeted him.

The air seemed to crackle around him when he walked into the living room. His features seemed chiseled out of stone, harder than Tamara had ever seen them.

"A little," Bick admitted tersely as the fierce green of his eyes was directed at her once and flicked immediately away.

"The mail is on the coffee table." She pointed to the stack of letters sitting near her purse. She had never seen him this tense. "You look as if you had a rough day at the office. Would you like a drink?" she suggested, and rose from the couch to pour him one.

Bick didn't refuse or agree, so Tamara took his silence as an affirmative, walking to the liquor tray on a side table.

"How's your mother today?"

She almost said fine, but that wasn't the truth. "She's slipping." Removing the stopper from the decanter, she poured a splash of liquor into a crystal glass. "It's happening so gradually that you don't notice until you realize that something she could do last week, she can't do this week."

"You'd realize it if you only visited her once a week. How often do you see your mother?"

"Every day. You know that." Tamara laughed at the ridiculous question and lifted the lid of the ice bucket.

"Where did you get this money? From your mother?"

The question and his savage tone of voice made Tamara look over her shoulder. He was standing by the coffee table, holding her opened purse in one hand and bills in the other.

She turned sharply to demand in outrage, "What are you doing in my purse? You have no right to go through my things!"

"I want to know how you came by this money!" His fingers crumpled the money into his fist as he exploded. "And, dammit, don't lie to me because I saw you in the hotel this afternoon! I wondered what you were doing for money. I couldn't believe you still had any left out of your last paycheck. This afternoon gave me a pretty damned good idea of where you're getting it!"

Tamara stiffened at his snarling rage and ugly insinuation. Anger began trembling through her. "I earned it!" she flared.

His nostrils widened to drink in an angry breath as his mouth curled in a sneer. "I'll just bet you did!"

As if he couldn't stand the sight of her, Bick spun away, an arm knocking over the lamp on an end table. It fell with a crash, the porcelain vase cracking open. But he didn't even glance at it, taking a long stride that carried him to the back of an occasional chair. His hands gripped the top of it, fingers digging into the soft upholstery while he lowered his head to stare at the floor.

At first, Tamara was speechless at the interpretation he had made from her answer. She stared at him, brutally hurt and incapable of hurting back. She moved toward him like an automaton.

"Aren't you going to ask me how I earned that money?" she demanded hoarsely. Standing behind him and to one side, Tamara could see the muscles working convulsively along his jaw, but he didn't answer. "You ask me!" she cried in frustration, and grabbed at his arm to make him look at her.

Bick shook off the attempt and countered it by gripping her wrist. "I could almost kill you for this," he warned.

Tamara was too incensed to be threatened by the ominous gleam in his eyes. "I earned that money typing! Typing for some of the same people who used to hire me before! It gives me spending money and helps pass the time while Mother is resting!" she told him angrily, and jerked her wrist free of his hold. "That's what I was doing today in that hotel! Delivering some envelopes I had addressed for the hotel's convention center! But I don't expect you to take my word for it!" She pivoted away to stalk to the telephone extension in the living room and lifted the receiver to offer it to him. "You call the hotel yourself. Ask them if they know me! Ask them if I do typing for them on occasion!" Tamara challenged.

At that moment the housekeeper came bustling in the room, clicking her tongue at the broken lamp on the floor. She began picking up the pieces scattered in the thick shag of the carpet. The intrusion was more than Tamara would tolerate.

"You order her out of this room, Bick Rutledge," she demanded.

His gaze skipped to the housekeeper. "You can clean it up later, Freyda."

"It will only take a moment." The housekeeper didn't pause in her task.

"Leave it!" Bick snapped.

"Very well." The woman gave in with ill grace and walked stiffly from the room.

"Aren't you going to call?" Tamara demanded with the telephone receiver still in her hand. "No, of course not," she realized. "You'll wait until you get to your office tomorrow to check out my 'story.'"

Bick ignored her sarcastic jibe. "Why didn't you ask me for some money?"

"You have to be kidding." The huskiness of anger remained in her voice although much of the heat of it had burned off. "I don't want to be dependent on you for every penny. And asking you only invites insults that make me feel cheap.''

"You aren't cheap. You should take a look at some of the checks I've written lately and you'd know you haven't been a bargain!" he flared.

"It always comes back to money, doesn't it?" Tamara murmured in a low, taut voice.

"Why didn't you tell me you were typing to earn money? Why was it such a secret?" Bick demanded.

"I don't have to tell you every single thing I do. As it is, you make me feel like I'm being held hostage for twenty thousand dollars," she protested. "And it isn't fair!"

"You aren't staying here against your will," he stated, and released a hard laugh. "As a matter of fact, there isn't an unwilling bone in your body!"

He started across the room toward her. The unwavering grimness of his look warned Tamara that he intended to prove his statement. She took a step backward and bumped against a table. Before she could move sideways out of his path, his hand was snaring her arm and pulling her back.

"No!" The animal cry of protest came from her throat as she struggled and struck out at him.

She was hauled against his chest, his strength overpowering her. The few of her blows that landed glanced harmlessly off his muscled frame. He pinned her arms to her sides and scooped her kicking legs into the air. Tamara twisted and strained violently as he carried her out of the living room down the hall to the master bedroom.

Kicking the door shut, he crossed the room to drop her on the bed. Before she could roll to the other side, Bick was there to pull her back, pinning her to the mattress with his crushing weight. When she tried to turn away from the assault of his mouth, he grabbed a handful of hair and forced her surrender. But Tamara continued to resist, her hands straining to push at his chest while her legs tried to wiggle out of the scissors grip of his.

"You brute! Let me go!" Her protest was a hoarse burst of impotence and frustration.

"You don't want me to make love to you?" Bick murmured against her throat.

"No."

"Like hell you don't." He bruised her mouth with his lips, then lifted his head to add a taunting, "I can feel you trembling."

It was true, Tamara realized. An inflaming heat was spreading through her skin, melting her resistance even as she tried not to weaken.

"Bick, you're hurting me." It was hard to breathe with the weight of his chest crushing her lungs.

He eased the pressure of his pinning weight and the force of his kiss became persuasive. "You deserve to be punished after the agony I went through this afternoon when I saw you in that hotel."

"You shouldn't have jumped to such an awful conclusion without talking to me first," Tamara replied in a voice that quivered from the delicious havoc his lips were creating. "That wasn't fair."

His hands began seeking out her curves. "Where is it written in our marriage contract that I have to be fair?'' he questioned softly. ''Is it fair the way you tangle me in knots? You get near me and I can't tell black from white.''

It became a wondrous struggle to prove who affected the other more. When it was over, Tamara didn't know whether she had won or lost. It didn't really matter, she decided, and snuggled closer against Bick, watching the play of her fingers over the muscled tautness of his shoulder.

''I've decided what we're going to do for the rest of the evening,'' Bick murmured as he nuzzled her ear.

''What?'' She turned her head on the pillow to look at him, forcing Bick to abandon his idle munching.

While his green eyes roamed sexily over her face, his hand glided across her stomach to cup the fullness of a breast in its palm. ''We're going to spend it right here in this bed—unless you have a better idea.''

''Not a one,'' Tamara admitted.

He shifted to remove his arm from beneath her shoulders and take the pillow from beneath her head. The movement slipped the satin sheet lower on his hips as he bent over her.

''One more thing, though.'' He kissed the corner of her mouth. ''I don't want you doing any more typing for anybody. I'll give you an allowance so you can have some spending money.''

''No.'' That spark of independence flared in her look. ''I don't want you to give me anything.''

''You don't?''

Tamara was surprised to see amusement twitching his mouth when she expected anger. ''No, I don't,'' she replied warily.

"You don't want me to give you...*anything?*" The suggestive pause was deliberate and heavy with passionate implication.

It caught at her breath. Bick didn't have to wait for an answer because it was written in her look. "You know what I meant," she whispered.

"Then show me what you didn't mean," he challenged, and opened his mouth on her lips.

The kiss had just begun to deepen and flame with the portent of what was to come when there was a sharp knock at their bedroom door, catching them both by surprise. Bick struggled for a normal breath.

"Yes, what is it?" he demanded and frowned at the interruption.

No permission had been granted to enter but the knob was being turned anyway. Swearing under his breath, Bick pulled the sheet over Tamara and elevated himself on an elbow to glare at the housekeeper. There were pinched lines of disapproval in her expression at finding them in bed at this hour of the day, but no embarrassment.

"I beg your pardon," she said insincerely, "but there is a gentleman on the telephone for you. I couldn't understand his name because his accent was much too thick."

"Hans!" Bick breathed in the name and glanced sharply at his watch. "My God, we were supposed to meet him for dinner five minutes ago!" He stretched across Tamara to pick up the telephone extension on the bedside table while the housekeeper silently withdrew. The telephone cord was too short and Bick had to remain angled across her, a position neither of them minded. "Hello, Hans? . . . Yes, we're running a little bit late. What? . . ." A smile touched his mouth as he glanced at Tamara. "I had a family matter that demanded my attention, but we'll be there in about twenty minutes." After saying goodbye, he reached over to replace the receiver on the hook, then paused above her. "I forgot I promised we would join him for dinner."

"I guess that means we'll have to cancel our previous plans." She sighed and half-smiled in regret.

"We'll take a raincheck for tomorrow night."

"I might have a headache tomorrow night," she suggested playfully.

"I'll have the cure." He claimed her mouth in a long, sensuous kiss to prove his self-confidence wasn't misplaced, but her response was more than he had bargained for, and he dragged his mouth from hers with an effort. "Tamara, we're going to be late."

She lifted a hand to trace the outline of his mouth, warm from the kiss. "I can't get out of bed until you move," she reminded him with infuriating logic.

His hand captured the fingers teasing his mouth and slammed them to the mattress beside her head. He did the same with the other hand and pinned both to the mattress above her head. With his position of dominance established, his gaze suddenly glazed with the knowledge.

"Hell, what does it matter if we're thirty minutes late?" he muttered thickly and lowered his head to show her how they were going to spend the extra minutes.

As it turned out, they were forty-five minutes late arriving at the hotel. Hans Zimmer was polite enough not to point out the fact to them. Although the German field representative spoke in a monotonous voice and wrestled with the English language, Tamara was entertained by his witty and astute observations about the United States, which kept the social–business evening from dragging.

While they were having coffee, the man in charge of the conventions held at the hotel stopped by the table to thank Tamara for being so prompt with the typing. At Bick's invitation, he stayed to have a cup of coffee with them. During the short but friendly conversation he had with Bick, the man unconsciously confirmed everything Tamara had said.

But having her story proved true wasn't any consolation for her. Tamara was aware that Bick's remarks had invited the confirmation or a denial, because he hadn't completely believed her. When the man left, Tamara took a sip of coffee that had suddenly become very bitter.

Lowering her voice so their German table companion wouldn't overhear what she said, she murmured to Bick, "Now you won't have to waste precious time tomorrow calling the hotel to confirm what I was doing here, will you?"

He flashed her a silencing look, but she knew she was right. And it hurt.

Chapter Nine

Bick awakened slowly and turned to look at his bed partner. The drowsy remnants of sleep vanished from his eyes at the empty pillow beside his. His gaze began a swift arc of the room and stopped abruptly at the sight of Tamara sitting on the sofa with her legs tucked beneath her, leaning over the backrest to gaze out the window.

"You're awake kind of early this morning, aren't you?" He tossed back the covers and swung out of bed.

"I woke up and couldn't go back to sleep," she responded absently without turning to look at him.

It had happened several times in recent days, Bick remembered. He had already guessed the cause, since her mother's condition had deteriorated rapidly in the past two weeks. He had noticed when he had paid his regular visit on Saturday. Now Tamara was beginning to lose sleep because of it, but he had been reluctant to discuss it with her, not wanting to upset her more.

But it bothered him the way Tamara sat staring out the window while he dressed, as if maintaining some silent vigil. He walked to the sofa and laid a hand on her shoulder. Other than a downward glance at his hand, she didn't move.

"Worried about your mother?" he asked gently.

Pressing her lips together, she gave him a hesitant nod of affirmation. The action let him see the pale and weary look of her face. Bick was glad of the distraction since he couldn't think of a single word to offer her in comfort.

"You are beginning to look peaked," Bick observed. "In addition to all this worrying, you aren't still doing typing as well?"

"Yes, I am." There was no hesitation in her answer. Despite the time that had passed, it was still a sore subject between them.

"Give it up, Tamara," he urged. "You are putting too much pressure on yourself. Considering how much money I've already spent on your behalf, what difference does it make if I give you an allowance too?" As soon as it was out, Bick knew he had put his foot in his mouth again. He wanted to kick himself.

Stiffly she uncurled her legs and rose from the couch. "I don't want to discuss it." She walked away from him, her fingers nervously linked in front of her. "You'd better go have your breakfast or you'll be late."

Bick hesitated, wanting to undo the damage he'd done—but how? Impatient that he found no answer, he left the room. How in the world did he run a national corporation when he couldn't even manage his wife? The answer to that one he had. With Tamara, he was emotionally involved and vulnerable.

The incident plagued him all morning. Before leaving for lunch, he told Mrs. Davies to cancel all his appointments after three o'clock. He had decided to leave the office early and pick up Tamara at her mother's so she wouldn't have that long bus ride home. Maybe he could buy her a present—or take her out to dinner. The latter sounded the wisest. It wouldn't be misinterpreted.

He was clearing his desk to leave when Mrs. Davies rang through. "There is a Ms. Kent on line one. She says it's urgent."

Bick immediately switched over to the call. "Sadie. Is anything wrong?"

"Yes, I'm afraid so. It's Lucretia—Mrs. James."

He could hear the emotion choking her voice. "I'll be right over," He promised grimly.

"Do you...do you know where Tamara is? I called the house but she isn't there. And I—"

"Do you mean she isn't with her mother—with you?" he said incredulously.

"No. She was here for an hour or so in the morning, then left. Don't you know where she is either?" He could hear the panic in the nurse's voice.

"Don't worry. I'll find her," Bick promised without knowing whether he could fulfill it or not. "We'll come as soon as we can."

Hanging up the phone, he began swearing. She had to be delivering some of that damned typing, he reasoned. And he had absolutely no idea who she typed for or where she might be. The only certainty was that she would return to the house. So that's where he would go.

When he arrived, Tamara hadn't returned. He called Sadie in case Tamara showed up there and left word where he was. He made a half dozen futile calls and began pacing the floor. Freyda hadn't been able to offer anything beyond the fact that she thought Tamara had gone to her mother's.

It was the longest half hour he had ever spent before he heard the front door open. Bick was in the foyer before it closed. The waiting, not knowing where Tamara was, had worn his temper thin.

"Where have you been?" he barked out the demand, startling the smile from her face. "I have been trying to find you for an hour! The next time you are going to let people know where you are going. And you are doing no more typing! That's it. This finishes it!"

"I will do what I please," she murmured stiffly, and started to walk past him.

It hit Bick that he had to break the news to her about her mother. "Tamara, wait." His voice was quieter, gentler. There was wary confusion in her look, an inability to adjust to his abrupt change in attitude. "Sadie called me at the office. She wants us to come."

Tamara made no sound, but she went white as a sheet. Bick thought she was going to faint and was instantly at her side, putting an arm around her hunched shoulders, murmuring over and over again that he was sorry. But she gathered herself together, although she accepted the support of his arm as he walked her to the car.

When they arrived at the house, Tamara went immediately to her mother's bedside. The woman was conscious but not very lucid. Sadie was trying to keep a professional front, but there were tears in her eyes. The doctor came over to confer with Bick.

"Is there nothing that can be done?" He guessed the doctor's answer even before he asked the question, his gaze riveted on Tamara.

"Nothing that would reverse the course of her condition. And Mrs. James left written instructions that her life not be artificially maintained." On that, the doctor lifted his shoulders in an expressive shrug. "I understand there is coffee in the kitchen. I'm going to have a cup. Would you care to join me?"

"No." Bick shook his head. He wanted to be here with Tamara.

It was a somber scene. The minutes ticked by slowly, every second lingering. When Tamara glanced at him over her shoulder, he automatically took a step toward her. He felt her stress, the unbearable pain and tension, as keenly as if it were his own.

"Mother...wants to speak to you," she told him, and moved away from the bed so he could take her place.

After casting an anxious eye over Tamara, Bick walked to the bed. "I'm here, Mother James."

She said something, but her voice was so weak, it was barely a whisper. He had to bend close to hear her. Even then he only caught snatches of sentences.

"... no insurance. I cashed in the policy ... worried so much. I wanted her ... the money when she needed it ... didn't   tell ... inheritance.   Maybe ... needs more ... after I'm gone. Thought I was ... right. Explain to her."

Bick could fill in the parts he missed, enough to understand that Mrs. James was confirming Tamara's story. Frustration seized him that he hadn't asked her before, but he knew why he hadn't. They could have collaborated.

"Did Tamara ask you to tell me this?" His question was very low and very sharp. "Was this her idea?" He hated himself for asking, but he had to know.

Between her slurring voice and the weakness of its volume, he lost the first part of her words. Her eyes were closed and Bick couldn't tell if she had actually heard his question. He caught a word—*babies*—or had she said "my baby," referring to Tamara.

"She said you didn't ..." Bick didn't hear the rest of the sentence. He could only surmise that the last of it might have been "believe her—she said you didn't believe her." He glanced up as Sadie moved to the other side of the bed.

"Sh ... She's unconscious now," the nurse murmured.

The statement brought a gasp from Tamara. She hurried to the bed and Bick stepped aside. His mouth was tight and grim as Tamara grasped her mother's hand tightly, as if holding on.

"Mama, can you hear me?" Her voice wavered, but it was otherwise calm. "Mama?" There was no response. "Mama, I'm going to have a baby. The doctor told me today. Mama?"

Stunned, Bick couldn't immediately register her words. Part of him wasn't even sure he had understood her correctly. It solved the mystery of where Tamara had been that day.

"I think she heard you," Sadie murmured. "She . . . tried to smile."

Then the doctor was in the room, nodding silently to Bick in a signal to escort Tamara away from the bed. She resisted the touch of his hands for only a second, then walked with him to the foot of the bed. Standing behind her, he kept a hand on her waist. He could feel she was stiff, braced for these next moments to come. Gently, he eased her back until her shoulders were resting against his chest. His hand slid to the front of her stomach to hold her there. A tingling awe splintered through him at the life that was beneath his hand. There was a slight exploring of his fingers as if he expected to feel movement or a heartbeat—some confirmation of their baby.

"Is it true? What you said about the baby?" Bick murmured near her ear.

Her hand moved to cover his hand pressed gently to her flat stomach. "Yes," she nodded. He felt her relax slightly in his arms.

Unable to draw the waistband closed on the pair of slacks, Tamara took them off and looked for a pair with an elastic waistband. She found a blue pair and pulled them on. They were a little tight but at least they went around her, which was more than the majority of her clothes did.

Turning sideways, she studied her silhouette in the mirror. There was a bulging roundness to her stomach that went with her thickening waist. Her breasts were becoming fuller. She was definitely beginning to show that she was with child.

What with the funeral and sorting through her mother's personal possessions and making decisions about the rest and a little natural grieving, Tamara hadn't had much time this past month to adjust to this change within her. Nor was she altogether sure how Bick felt about it.

Naturally she had discussed it with him to some degree—assured him that the doctor said she was perfectly healthy, the baby was due in February—things like that. But whether he wanted it as much as she did was something Tamara didn't know. He seemed happy about it, concerned about her, sometimes treating her like a piece of delicate porcelain.

If he wasn't overly jubilant, Tamara preferred to think it was out of respect for her mourning. He had been her rock through it all. His arms had consoled her grief and his kisses had given her back the joy in living. When she didn't cry, Bick hadn't suggested she should. When she did cry, he didn't tell her to stop.

A smile touched her mouth as she remembered what a gentle but very passionate lover he could be. Turning from the mirror, Tamara stopped when she saw Bick had come in from the bathroom. There was every indication that he had been watching her for some time.

"I'm putting on weight," she said to explain why she was looking at herself in the mirror.

"Yes, you are." He moved forward and she reached to put on her blouse. One arm was in the sleeve when his hands circled her from behind to cross and hold a breast. "And in all the right places for a pregnant lady," he murmured against her hair.

"I should hope so," she laughed, and pushed out of his arms to finish putting on her blouse.

"Why did you get pregnant? I never have asked."

"What kind of a question is that?" She laughed again, sending him an amused glance as she buttoned her blouse. Despite the half-smile on his mouth, she could see he was serious. And she no longer felt amused. "Why am I the one who did it? What about you and your virility? You had a part in this, too." She walked to her dresser and picked up the hairbrush.

"I am aware of that," he said dryly.

"If you are aware of it, then why didn't you do something to prevent it?" she challenged. "Why was it my responsibility?"

"I never said it was yours," Bick corrected, coming to stand behind her. "I was merely wondering what made you decide you wanted to have a baby." He let a handful of her hair slide through his fingers and watched the rippling, silver-gold effect the light made on it. "Did you hope a child would tie you to me forever? Or were you making sure I would have reason to provide for you the rest of your life in the event of a divorce?"

Stung by his questions, Tamara whirled around to challenge him with a defiant look. "Pick whichever one you want. Either reason will do! Naturally it would never occur to you that I might want the baby for the same reason that any other woman wants to have one. That would be much too simple!'' She was fighting tears by the time she had finished and attempted to turn away.

Bick caught her shoulders. ''I shouldn't have asked those questions. I don't know why I did.'' He gathered her close and she could almost feel the violent war raging within him.

''No, you shouldn't have,'' she agreed, and relaxed slightly, because she knew that part of him meant it.

''I'll tell you what we will do. Today is Saturday. Why don't we go shopping for some baby things, furnish the nursery? Would you like that?''

Tamara agreed because she knew it was an attempt to make up for the hurt he'd caused. She forgave him, but she knew she would never be able to forget what he'd said. After all this time, he still didn't believe in her. For a hopeless moment she wondered if he ever would.

The chair was sitting sideways to the library desk. It was the only way Tamara could sit in it and write on the desktop. She crossed off another name on the Christmas card list and reached for the next envelope to address. She tossed a quick glance to the window, but it was dark outside, turning the windowpanes into mirrors.

A shadow fell into the room from the hallway an instant before Bick said, ''So this is where you are hiding.''

"I was just about to decide you were going to be late." She set the stack of cards aside for a later time.

"I had a stop to make on the way home. Come on." He held out his hand to her. "I have a surprise for you."

Taking her by the hand, he led her to the master bedroom, where a gift-wrapped package sat on the bed. "What is it?" she asked.

"Open it and find out."

After untying the bow, she stripped away the foil paper to reveal a box. When she lifted the lid, she saw a cranberry-colored maternity dress resting in folds of tissue.

"It's beautiful," Tamara declared as she lifted it out of the box.

"With all the holiday entertaining we will be obligated to do, I thought you might need it," Bick explained. "Try it on."

Tamara needed no second urging. Bick had to fasten the hook at the back of the neckline. Then she stepped in front of the mirror. A network of hand-sewn cranberry beads formed the empire waistline and scrolled a border for the jewel neckline. It was softly draping and elegantly simple.

"How does it fit?" Bick asked.

"Like it was made for me. How did you manage it?" she murmured.

"I walked into a shop and told the saleslady I wanted a dress so wide"—he held his hands apart to indicate narrow shoulders—"and so big." He stretched his arms much farther apart to indicate the size of her stomach.

"Thanks a lot, but I'm not that big," she insisted in self-defense. Lifting her hair aside, she offered her back to him. "Unfasten the hook. I'd better take it off before I mess it up."

"No. Leave it on. I'm taking you out to dinner tonight," he stated, and lightly kissed the curve of her neck.

"You are?" Tamara turned in surprise.

"Yes. I thought we'd go to the Plaza, see the Christmas lights, and have dinner at a restaurant there. How does that sound?" Bick smiled lazily.

"Wonderful," she agreed. "Let me change shoes."

The Plaza was unique—the first shopping center in the United States, built in the early 1900s in the ornate Spanish style and heavily influenced by Moorish style. During the holiday season it became a fairyland, with its towers and domes and scalloped cornices outlined with bright lights. Strings of lights followed the streets and wound around the fountains. The store windows of the many shops glittered with lights and Christmas decorations. Tamara had a clear view of it all from a window seat in a restaurant atop one of the Plaza hotels. It was breathtaking.

"Beautiful, isn't it?" Bick offered his opinion.

"Very." She turned from the view to look across the table at her husband of eight months, a man who still hadn't told her those three simple words—"I love you." "You never did explain what I owe all this to. This dress . . . dinner . . ."

"I have to fly to Palm Springs on Monday," he admitted.

"For how long?" She twirled her water glass and took a sip, pretending she didn't mind.

"I should be back Thursday, maybe Wednesday. It's a business meeting." Bick sipped from a glass of wine.

"Of course." And she did believe him.

"It was scheduled for January, but I had it changed," he added. "That's too close to when the baby's due."

"The doctor said everything's going perfectly." She changed the subject to rid her mind of its vision of Bick strolling by a California pool with beautiful bikini-clad girls parading for him. It made her too self-conscious about her own swollen figure.

The conversation between them was vaguely stilted, as if each were trying to guard what was said. They tried to keep to safe, noncontroversial topics.

Halfway through the meal, Bick murmured very softly, "Well, well." Tamara glanced up to see he was rising to greet someone. "Hello, Frank. I didn't expect to see you here."

"I could say the same for you, Bick." A polished, crisp young man shook hands with Bick. He seemed to have stepped out of an advertisement for the ideal, rising young executive with his gold-rimmed glasses and three-piece suit. "I must not have seen you when you came in or I would have asked you to join us. My wife and I are with another couple sitting at a table across the way."

"That would have been generous of you." Bick smiled, but Tamara recognized that skeptical gleam in his eyes. "But we wouldn't have wanted to intrude on your party. Besides, my wife and I are enjoying one of our rare evenings alone. For that reason alone, I probably would have refused your invitation. I don't believe you have met my wife."

"No, I haven't had the pleasure." The man turned and smiled at her, but Tamara had the feeling she was being examined under a microscope.

"Tamara, this is Frank Shavert. He is with the legal staff. You know his uncle, Gil Shavert, one of our directors."

"Of course," she nodded. "How do you do, Mr. Shavert."

"May I present my wife, Tamara Rutledge," Bick finished.

"I have heard a great deal about you, Mrs. Rutledge, but no one has managed to convey how very beautiful you are." He bowed slightly at the waist.

"You are very kind." For some reason she wasn't flattered by the compliment.

"I understand you are flying to Palm Springs, Bick."

"Yes, on Monday," he admitted.

"I imagine sunny California will be a welcome change from chilly Kansas City."

"No doubt it will."

"I won't keep you from your meal. You're welcome to join us for coffee when you're finished," the man invited politely.

"I think not," Bick said, refusing.

Frank Shavert didn't argue. "Have a safe flight." With a nod to Tamara, he added, "Again, it was a pleasure meeting you at last."

Bick watched him walk away before sitting down in his chair to finish his meal. Tamara noticed the preoccupied and thoughtful look in his expression. As if feeling her gaze, he glanced at her.

"You just met the man who is being groomed to take my place, if his uncle has his way," he murmured dryly.

"How could he do that?"

"I have inherited my mother's stock in the company, but by no means do I have control." His gaze wandered in the direction of Frank Shavert's table. "Some day I'm going to be in for a proxy fight." At the flash of concern in her expression, a smile smoothed up the corners of his mouth. "Don't worry. It won't be for a while. Frank isn't ready yet. Besides, I don't intend to lose the fight."

"I can't imagine you losing," Tamara admitted.

His gaze ran warmly over her. "Neither can I." This time his smile was a genuine one.

"If Gil Shavert wants you out, why is he always having you over to his house? I thought he was your friend."

"No. But you have to be close to a person in order to stab them in the back—a case of *'Et tu, Brute.'*"

"Bick—"

"Don't worry," he repeated. "I'll know about it before they make a move."

She suddenly understood that he had to be naturally suspicious. In his own way, Bick had been taught not to trust. If he wanted to survive at the top, he had to be doubly wary of everybody's motives. What chance did she have?

When they had finished their main course, the waiter came to clear away their plates and returned to offer them dessert. A wicked light danced in Bick's green eyes.

"Dessert, Tamara? Don't you have a craving for pickles and strawberries?" he asked in teasing reference to her condition.

"No," she replied. "Nothing, thank you," she told the waiter.

"And you, sir? Dessert? Coffee?" the waiter inquired.

"Nothing. You may bring the check," Bick instructed.

"Very good, sir."

When the waiter had left, Bick glanced at his watch. "I'm in favor of going home. What about you?"

"Yes," Tamara agreed. Tonight had brought some revelations that she wanted to think over.

Tamara went to the powder room while Bick took care of the check. When she came out, he had collected her coat from the check room and was waiting for her near the exit to the elevators. He helped her into it and lifted the curtain of flaxen hair out of the inside of her furred collar.

"It's cold outside," he said as he turned her to fasten the top button of her coat. "I don't want you getting chilled."

With a complete disregard for the publicness of the restaurant, he bent to brush his mouth over hers. The feather-soft contact held a heady promise of something more satisfying to come. A breathless excitement fluttered her pulse.

"I think you have every intention of keeping me warm," Tamara murmured, fascinated by the man who still thrilled her with his touch.

"Do you object?" His gaze probed deeply behind half-closed lashes.

"On the contrary." Unconsciously she swayed toward him and his hands were on her shoulders to steady her and silently remind her of where they were.

Near them, a woman's voice asked, "Did you see Mrs. Rutledge when we walked by their table, Donna? She is beautiful."

The spreading fronds of a potted plant hid Tamara and Bick from the view of the woman, but her voice carried plainly. The unsolicited compliment about his wife brought a smile to Bick's face.

"She is very beautiful," came the second woman's response.

"They are right," Bick whispered huskily as neither made any attempt to make their presence known. "You are very beautiful." Tamara would have been content to bask in the reflection of the warm light shining from his eyes the rest of her life. Bick made her feel warm and beautiful and totally woman. But he was so totally male.

A man's voice inserted itself in the discussion of Tamara by the two women. "And very beautifully pregnant she is, too." Tamara recognized that smooth, educated voice as belonging to Frank Shavert. "That woman knows every trick in the book," he added on a contemptuous note, and Tamara stiffened.

"What do you mean?" There was avid curiosity in the first woman's question.

"She was nothing but a bookkeeper in a two-bit firm we absorbed," Frank continued, and Tamara watched Bick's lazy look narrow with cold anger. "But she knew all about balance sheets and bank statements. It's not surprising she saw dollar signs when she met Rutledge."

"What happened?"

Tamara was rooted to the floor, her stomach turning with a sickening rush. Bick's hands were biting into her shoulders, but she knew he wasn't aware of the pressure he was exerting. A cold, ruthless fury was building in his features, turning them to granite before her eyes.

"First, she conned Bick into paying back an alleged loan this firm had made her. Then there was a quickie wedding, supposedly because of her sick mother," Frank went on. "Obviously Rutledge got her pregnant and she forced him into marrying her. But she's going to produce an heir, which means she'll get her share of the Rutledge fortune, one way or another."

Tamara saw the fury rising up to explode as Bick started to push her aside to confront the man. "Bick, no," she protested.

His hard gaze slashed across her face. "He isn't going to get away with insulting you like that—not in my presence." His low voice vibrated with the implied threat of violence.

The irony of the situation pulled the corners of her mouth into a bitter smile. "Don't be a hypocrite. There wasn't anything he said that you haven't said or thought about me already," Tamara mocked. "If the truth were known, you are only angry because he's made you sound like a fool. Now your pride is demanding satisfaction.''

''No!'' Bick denied that immediately.

An overwhelming weariness swept over her. Her hand fluttered across her face to rest on the top of her stomach. ''Please take me home, Bick. I'm very tired.''

It was the truth. She was utterly weary of fighting his doubts and suspicions, of struggling for every scrap of his respect and affection. She ached all over from her many scars received in these battles.

The voices had already drifted out of their hearing. Bick wavered for a second more, then slid a hand to her elbow to escort her out of the restaurant. The silence between them lasted all the way to the house.

Once inside, Tamara didn't waste time with polite chitchat and simply announced, ''I'm going to bed.'' All the strength and determination had been drained from her voice, leaving it flat and lifeless.

No objection came from Bick, but he didn't follow her. For the first time that she could remember, Tamara hadn't wanted him to. She undressed in a weary daze and crawled into bed.

''Here's your lunch, Mrs. Rutledge.'' The housekeeper entered the living room carrying a tray.

Tamara glanced up from the crossword puzzle in her lap and viewed the soup, sandwich, and glass of milk with disinterest. ''I'm not hungry, Freyda. Thank you.'' The woman ignored her statement and set the tray on the coffee table. Tamara was already moody and her temper flared at the way the housekeeper constantly ignored her wishes. "I said I wasn't hungry. Now take it away," she ordered curtly.

"Mr. Rutledge left instructions that I was to make certain you ate properly while he was gone," the woman stated.

"Mr. Rutledge isn't here. He's in Palm Springs." But the admonition prompted Tamara to remove the glass of milk from the tray. "Now take it away."

The housekeeper sniffed and picked up the tray. "I can't be accused of not providing you nourishing food. If you don't want to eat it, I have better things to do with my time than argue with you."

"Precisely my opinion," Tamara retorted.

As the housekeeper carried the tray away, she tried to turn her attention back to the crossword puzzle, but it had lost its interest. With an irritated movement, she tossed the paper on the coffee table and took a drink of the milk. It tasted like chalk and was cast aside too. She glanced at the phone, wondering if Bick would call her as he had done yesterday.

Only once had he referred to the incident in the restaurant and that was to ask her the following morning if she was still angry with him for almost creating a scene. Naturally, Tamara had denied that because she hadn't been angry with him. Not even his love-making since had been able to erase the feeling of dejection that had lingered. On the surface she had tried to pretend to him that nothing had changed, but inside it had.

The doorbell rang and Tamara shifted into a position where she could maneuver herself upright. It rang again before she reached the door. When she opened the door, she recognized the short, rotund man as the attorney Bick had engaged to settle the legal side of her mother's affairs.

"Hello, Mr. Sutton." Tamara smiled because his bright red cheeks and snowy hair reminded her of Santa Claus. Then she felt the invading draft of cold winter air. "Won't you come in?" She swung the door open wider to admit him.

"Thank you, Mrs. Rutledge." He swept off his hat as he stepped into the house. "How are you today?"

"Very well, thank you. May I take your coat?" she offered. After unwrapping the scarf from around his neck, he shrugged his round frame out of the heavy topcoat and handed it to her. Tamara walked over to hang it in the foyer coat closet. "I suppose you have some more papers for me to sign."

"It will be the last of them. I promise."

"Shall we go into the living room?" At his nod she led the way and sat in the chair she had recently vacated, while the attorney opened his briefcase to remove a sheaf of papers.

He went over the documents with her and explained the legal jargon. Tamara tried to listen attentively, but she wasn't really interested. She smiled and nodded as if she understood everything he said, but her thoughts were straying to other things. In a summation sheet, he showed her the itemized list of what had been derived from the sale of her mother's house, its furnishings, and the household goods. Another sheet listed the outstanding debts to be deducted.

"And I have a cashier's check here for you in the amount of the balance," Mr. Sutton concluded, and reached into his briefcase to hand it to her.

It was over three thousand dollars, and Tamara knew she had missed something. "How can this be? With all the mortgages, there couldn't have been this much equity in the house."

"That's true. But, as I mentioned, we found some articles packed away in the attic that were collector's items, and one or two pieces of furniture had antique value," he explained.

Had he said that? She didn't remember. "I guess I didn't expect it to add up to this much," she murmured.

"Since your family is expanding, I'm sure you'll find plenty of use for it." The attorney smiled benevolently.

"Yes . . . yes, I will," Tamara agreed.

"I'd better be getting back to my office," he stated. When Tamara started to rise, he held up a detaining hand. "No, don't get up. I can find my own way out."

"Thank you. Oh, I put your coat in the closet," she added. She was having trouble thinking about anything but the check in her hand.

"I'll find it. Have a good day, Mrs. Rutledge."

She nodded absently and never heard the front door open or close when he departed. The noise of the vacuum cleaner humming loudly from the dining room finally penetrated her thoughts. Folding the check in half, Tamara slipped it into the pocket of her maternity smock, an absent frown creasing her forehead. She was working the crossword puzzle again when the housekeeper glanced into the room.

In the middle of the afternoon, Bick called long distance from California. It was noon time there and he had only a few minutes before he had to keep a luncheon appointment. They talked but said little.

"I'll see you Thursday," he offered in goodbye, hesitated, then added, "Tamara, take care of yourself."

"I will," she promised. "Have a safe flight."

Such empty phrases, she thought as she hung up the phone. But that's the way it was always going to be. As long as Bick didn't trust her or believe her, he could never love her. Never was much too long a time.

Taking the check from her pocket, Tamara studied it again. Her first thought had been to sign it over to Bick as a partial payment for all the money he'd spent. But it was essentially an empty gesture, she realized, because she didn't have the means to pay the rest of it.

But the check could provide her with a new start in life . . . for her and the baby. It wouldn't be easy financially, because it wasn't that much. But she knew all about budgeting, living on a shoestring, and making do with very little.

If she was going to leave him, Tamara knew, she had to do it now, while Bick was too far away to take her in his arms and change her mind. She glanced at her watch. If she hurried, there was time to cash the check at the bank before it closed.

Chapter Ten

Resting her fingers on the typewriter keys, Tamara paused to arch her back and flex the cramping muscles. With the break in her concentration, she automatically glanced at the bassinet. A smile wiped the tiredness from her expression at the sight of the sleeping baby girl. A tiny fist waved the air.

"Are you telling me to get back to work, Lucy? You like the sound of the typewriter, don't you?" Tamara mused aloud.

The little fist flailed the air again, but Tamara didn't pay any attention to the order. She was enchanted by the doll-like baby wrapped in the yellow-flowered blanket—perfect little features complete in every detail, a mass of dark hair with a hint of red in it. A rush of maternal love engulfed Tamara.

There was a knock at the door of her one-room apartment. The baby stirred at the sharp sound and

Tamara hurried to answer the door. "I hope that's Mr. Claxton with that manuscript he wants typed," she murmured to the baby.

Keeping the chain on the door, she opened it a crack. A tall, burly man stood in the hallway outside. His jowled features reminded Tamara of a bulldog. He doffed his cowboy hat and peered at her through the narrow opening. He had a packet tucked under his arm, half hidden by his western-style jacket.

"I called you earlier about your ad in the Fort Worth paper," he said, and glanced at the number on her door. "I believe I have the right apartment."

"You are Mr. Claxton?" Tamara verified.

"That's right," he nodded.

She closed the door to unlatch the chain and let him in. "You have a manuscript you want typed?" she prompted as he stepped in and made a sweeping survey of the single-room apartment with its kitchenette, sofa bed, and chair.

"Here it is, Miss—" He handed her the packet and waited expectantly for her to furnish her name.

"*Mrs.* Rutledge." She stressed her marital status, noting the faintly surprised gleam in his eyes. "How soon will you want me to have this done?"

"There's no rush," he insisted. "Whenever you can."

Tamara opened the packet to see how long the manuscript was. "I can have it finished for you in a week."

"That's fine." His gaze was traveling around the room again.

"If you'll just give me a moment, I'll glance through it and see if I have any questions," she said.

"Of course," he agreed. Out of the corner of her eye, Tamara saw him walk to the bassinet. "A boy?"

"A girl," she corrected, and continued to leaf through the manuscript pages.

"My wife and I have three boys ourselves." He bent over the white basket but did nothing that would waken the sleeping infant. "I always wanted a little girl. How old is she?"

"Almost seven weeks."

"She's precious." The man straightened and walked to the table where Tamara was standing. He watched her for a moment. "How long have you been doing typing? I don't remember seeing your ad in the paper before."

"For quite some time now," she admitted without being exact.

"Are you from the Dallas-Fort Worth area originally?" He tipped his head to one side in a curious manner.

"I don't have the required accent, do I?" Laughter danced in her eyes. "I'm from Missouri originally. I moved here shortly before Christmas." She let the papers fall back into the box. "Everything seems very self-explanatory regarding your manuscript. I have a few pages to finish on this thesis. Then I'll be able to start on yours."

"Very good." He nodded. "I marked my telephone number on the first page. You can call me when you have it finished."

"I will, Mr. Claxton." She walked him to the door and locked it after him.

The next morning, Tamara got an early start on the manuscript. An empty glass sat beside her typewriter, a film of orange juice on the sides. A wisp of blond hair escaped from the ponytail to tickle her cheek. Tamara pushed it beneath the confining ribbon and resumed her place on the page. A hiccuping sob came from the baby basket followed by a second, then an outright wail began.

"Sssh, honey," Tamara murmured. "Mama knows you're hungry. Just give me a minute to finish this sentence."

But the angry crying didn't diminish in volume or impatience. Tamara hit the period key and moved quickly to pick up her squalling daughter.

"Can't you get your fist in your mouth, hm, Lucy?" she crooned. While Tamara was shifting the baby into the cradle of her arm, there was a sharp knock at the door. She started to ask who was there, but she wouldn't have heard the answer over Lucy's cries. She hurried to the door and opened it before she realized the safety chain wasn't on. By then she was looking into a pair of green eyes haunted with anxiety.

"What happened? Is she hurt?" Bick questioned.

Tamara stared at him for a long moment, unable to speak or move. A dark stubble shadowed his cheek and jaw, adding to his haggard and unkempt appearance. His chestnut hair was rumpled. Most incongruous of all was the pink and white teddy bear clutched in his hand. Her heart was beating so fast she couldn't think. Lucy's cries increased in volume and demand, pulling Tamara's mind back to his question.

"She's...just hungry." The urge to fling herself into his arms, baby and all, was almost irresistible. She turned away from the door to escape its power.

Aware that Bick followed her inside, Tamara began shaking so badly that she was afraid she was going to drop the baby. She laid her in the basket and walked to the kitchen area of the room. Remembering that Bick liked her hair down, she pulled the ribbon from her hair. She half-filled a baby bottle with warm water and screwed the nipple on, her action an instinctive response to the baby's crying.

When she turned from the sink, she saw Bick standing by the bassinet holding Lucy in his arms along with the teddy bear. Cold fear splintered through her. Had he come to take Lucy away from her?

"She's mine," Tamara stated. "You said I could have anything you gave me. You gave her to me, Bick." When she walked over to take the baby from him, he didn't resist. His gaze was riveted to Lucy's face, taking in every detail. "I . . . I named her Lucretia after my mother," she offered. "But I call her Lucy."

The crying stopped abruptly when the little mouth found the nipple of the bottle. After one swallow, Lucy rejected the taste of water and began crying again.

"Don't you have any milk?" Bick asked. "I'll go to the store for some."

"No." Tamara tried to tease Lucy into accepting the bottle—without success. "Formulas don't agree with her. I...I nurse her," she explained after a self-conscious hesitation, and Lucy continued to wail.

"She's hungry." Concern laced his voice.

"Yes, I know. I—" She realized she was being foolish and needlessly shy. Turning, she walked to the kitchen chair pushed up to the table where her type-writer sat. She pulled it out at right angles to the table and sat down. Lucy wanted nothing to do with the bottle of water, so Tamara set it upright on the table and unbuttoned her blouse. Within minutes, Lucy was nursing, greedily, tiny fingers kneading her breast. Tamara smoothed her daughter's soft brown hair with its red-gold highlights and smiled at its silken texture.

"Come home." The hoarse phrase lifted Tamara's gaze. Bick was sitting in the solitary armchair facing her. He was leaning forward, his elbows on his knees, the teddy bear clasped in both hands. Tears were shimmering in his eyes. "Have pity on me, Tamara, and come home."

"B...Because of the baby?" she asked, because that's all he had talked about since he'd arrived.

He seemed to struggle for the ability to speak. "If that's the only thing that will bring you back, then, yes, because of the baby."

"How did you know I was here? How did you find me?" she murmured.

"I've gone through hell these last four months trying to find you," Bick admitted on a thread of pain. "I've had every police department, every detective agency within a thousand miles of Kansas City looking for you. Finally Claxton picked up on the information that you used to do typing in your home. He started calling every ad in the newspaper."

"Claxton," she repeated. "He was here yesterday."

"Yes. He called to tell me he'd found you. I flew in yesterday afternoon. I spent last night at the bar on the corner—with this guy"—standing up, Bick tossed the teddy bear in the seat he'd vacated—"trying to get up enough courage to come up here. A half dozen times I made it all the way to your door, but... Finally I heard...Lucy crying, and I had to make sure you were all right." He turned away to rub at his eyes.

"I'm fine. We're both fine," she said.

After a moment of agitated hesitation, Bick walked over to crouch beside her chair, gazing at her with such longing that she wanted to die. "I know you said in the note you left that our marriage would never work, but give it another chance, Tamara."

"It's no use." It was the hardest thing in the world to say. "You don't trust me, Bick, you don't believe me. You are all filled with doubts about me."

"I was...once," he admitted grimly. "I had to hear someone else say all the things I had said. And the minute I looked at you, I knew they couldn't have been farther from the truth. Everything you told me was the truth. I know that now, Tamara."

"If you did, then why didn't you say so the night you heard Frank say all those things? Why didn't you tell *me?*" she protested.

"Because... I had to figure out why I was trying to hang on to all those doubts, why I didn't want to believe you. When I was in California, I realized that it was because I was so much in love with you, it scared the hell out of me. One person who could make me so happy—or torture me with endless pain. Oh, God, Tamara," he choked, "why did you leave me?"

"Because—" Her heart was soaring at his words. "Because I loved you so much that I couldn't bear it any more that you didn't love me. I . . . I came here to start a new life."

"Will you start a new life with me?" The emotion in his eyes implored her to agree.

"Yes. Yes!"

His arms went around her and the baby. "A new life for the three of us," he promised against her lips.

*   *   *   *   *